I0598715

CHOICE

JAMES GREEN

Choice/James Green

ISBN-13: 978-0615801940

ISBN-10: 061801943

DDA PUBLISHING

TABLE OF CONTENTS

PREFACE

This is the story of Christian L. Smith. He finds himself obsessed with searching for the truth about God, The Devil, and life itself. When in quest for something of that magnitude, eventually you are forced to make a choice.

This is a story about love, hate, murder and deception. Christian finds himself on a journey that there is no turning back from. It will be one he will never forget.

CHAPTER 1

If I had to put a time frame on it, I would say for about a year now I've been consumed with an obsession. People have all kinds of obsessions; clothes, shoes, makeup, even sex. This obsession of mine as cost me my girlfriend, the life of my best friend and most of all my sanity. My name is Christian L. Smith born October 31st 1986. My name sounds normal, average you could say. Its my middle name that sets me apart from the rest. It is my middle name that gives me the reason to tell you this story. My middle name is Lucifer. I never got the chance to ask my parents why they chose that name for me. My parents passed away when I was just a child.

Growing up I didn't have a lot of friends. Kids were always hesitant to talk to me or get to know me. Eventually I got used to being alone, it became comforting. Black was my favorite color. I wouldn't say that I dressed gothic or anything, but black was all I wore. My shirt, pants, underwear, socks and shoes, even my back pack were always black. Being well groomed and smelling nice was always important to me. If you asked me I would say I was pretty handsome. There was one, small, teeny tiny thing about me no one knew about.

Since I was a small child, I've always had a

presence with me. You know the feeling you

get when someone else is in the room with

you? Well mine was much more than that.

That chill that ran up my spine, the goose

bumps that covered my arm, it was all for

reason. That presence I felt, I could actually see

it. It didn't talk, usually it never moved. It

would only appear and disappear. I could feel

it all the time, but I usually never got to see it

until nightfall.

I still remember the first time I saw it. It

was the darkest, deepest, most horrendous fear

one could imagine. As time went on, my fear

subsided. Eventually, each night, I expected it

to be there. It may have been weird, but with it

there, I didn't feel so alone.

CHAPTER 2

When I was three years old, my parents died in a house fire. I still remember being carried out of the house by one of the firemen. Some how he got me out of there without a scratch. We finally made it outside; I could remember coughing a little from the smoke. I stood there, next to the man that saved my life as we watched the rest of the firemen take on the huge fire. He held my hand until the ambulance arrived. "It'll be ok son" he said as he rubbed my hair. Back then I was too young to understand fires or death. I figured I would see my mom and dad again when it was all over…but I never did. To this day no one ever figured out how the fire started.

I had a few photographic memories of my parents. I can't recall too many happy memories. My mom, nose to nose with me with tears in her eyes was always a vivid memory of mine. As much as she tried to hold the tears back the running mascara always gave it away. Honestly I can't recall too many memories of my parents ever interacting with one another.

I remember some of the ride in the ambulance on the way to the hospital. I was just a little kid so the paramedics were up in

arms. I woke up in the hospital wearing an

oxygen mask. Back then I didn't know what

that was but I was too scared to remove it. That

day was the first day I ever saw the shadowy

figure. It stood there in the corner of the room.

At first glance I thought it was my dad. He

didn't move or speak but just stood

there…watching me. Realizing it wasn't my

dad, I pulled the covers over my head hoping

it would just go away.

The next day a few men dressed in suits

entered my room. They talked amongst each

other but I couldn't make out what they were

saying. One might look at me for a second, smile then go back to talking to the other men. They all eventually left, no good byes or anything. They never returned after that, the only time someone came in my room was to feed me or to check the machines.

That same night I remember falling asleep watching cartoons. Not sure what time it was but sometime during the middle of the night I was awakened by small breeze that swooped through the room. I was so cold and scared. Not looking back at the corner where I first saw the figure, I tucked myself back under the covers until I was able to fall asleep again.

CHAPTER 3

The next morning, I was taken to a large house that I found some time later was an orphanage. "This is your room" a man said as we stood at the doorway. There was a full sized bed, a TV to watch and a night stand. I stood there with my little suitcase with a realization setting in…that I had seen my parents for the last time.

I lived in the orphanage for the rest of my childhood and years to come. I attended public school not too far from where I lived. An A and B student, I would always bring awards home for honor or merit roll and perfect attendance. There were other kids in the orphanage that didn't go to school and didn't seem too fond of my accomplishments. No one really talked to me, sometimes I could hear them talk amongst each other referring to me as "the nerd". It hurt my feelings a little, but honestly it didn't compare to losing my mother.

One day one of the kids decided to say something to me. Apparently he had had enough of me bringing home awards. He blocked me from entering my room. "What you got there nerd boy, another award!" he

said in his annoying mocking voice. "Um yea,
want to see it?" I gullibly asked. He took the
award from my hand, looking back at his
friends that stood across the hall. He looked
me dead in the eyes and ripped it in two;
tossed it to the ground and walked away. I
could hear the high fives and laughs he shared
with his friends. I remember the rage that
overcame me as clear as day. I wasn't afraid of
him, but I didn't want to hurt him. Frustrated I
kicked my door open stormed in and slammed
the door shut behind me. Sitting on my bed it
felt like I was about to explode. Sad, hurt,
pissed…I felt it all. My emotions felt so

uncontrollable tears began to form. Not a second later after the first tear fell I felt a familiar breeze pass through the room. Quickly I looked to the corner of my room but there was no figure. The only memory I had of the breeze was being afraid, ironically at that moment I felt comforted.

A few days later, I returned home from school and saw a poster hanging on the wall. "Missing child" it said. I looked closer at the picture and saw that it was the kid Tommy Snider…the same kid who so rudely, ripped my award. No one ever saw him again.

CHAPTER 4

Growing up I always enjoyed reading. It was an opportunity for me to escape the world. There were times I finished books in one day. As long as it was interesting, I would read it. There was one particular book I came across that sparked my interest unlike any other…The Holy Bible. I came across it at a book store, it was on sale and being displayed in the front of the store. It was different and I had never read it so I said what the hell.

I figured it would be a good opportunity to learn a few things. I was always confused about why there were so many religions, why people believed so many different things. There were different Gods, different practices, it all made me curious but I never had any one to talk to about it.

From the first page it began to contradict everything I had learned in school. How the universe came to be, how people came into existence. How was anyone supposed to know what the truth really was? If there was the possibility the Bible was wrong from page one what would be the point of reading it? I wondered.

I started reading the Bible my senior year in school. I'd read some during study hall, sometimes during lunch, I'd even sneak and read it during class if I found what we were learning to be not of interest. My grades were never a problem, I never worried about falling behind.

One day, my English teacher Ms. Kirkpatrick, caught me reading in the middle of class. I had already finished my pop quiz and decided to read while the others still tested. She walked up to me and took the book out of my hands. Looking at me strangely she handed it back "There's no time for that right now Christian. Take out your English book and start reading chapter 17 please. Your education should be your number one priority, remember that." Even in history class whenever I had a question about religion or God the teacher would avoid it and treated the subject as if it were off limits. The strangest thing of it all, whenever I read the Bible at home the figure never appeared. If it were already there, it would quickly disappear.

There were many times I tried to speak to it, hoping it would speak back. I didn't know what to say or ask outside of asking "who are you? What do you want from me?" It never responded. After a while the only dialogue was me saying hello when I entered the room or goodbye when I left.

As I read more and more of the Bible I ran across an interesting character by the name of Lucifer. I always thought my middle name was made up so when I saw it in the Bible it kind of excited me! Lucifer, it said, was the anointed cherub. I had no idea what that was so I had to do some research. It meant that he was set apart for God's divine purpose "bestowal of God's divine favor" God had given Lucifer authority and power in Heaven. He was made as a perfect being, the most beautiful and enchanted angel that was ever

created.

After reading that it gave an instant

gratification to my existence. It gave me a new

fond appreciation for my parents. They

thought enough of me to name me after the

most beautiful and powerful angel in heaven!

CHAPTER 5

To my surprise, I got a lot of female attention in school for a kid considered a nerd. Girls would always smile in passing, batting their eye lashes, sometimes even saying hello. Brad Manning, the captain of the football team didn't like the attention I was receiving. Ever since he earned the starting quarterback role his sophomore year he felt he was the king of Lockwood high. He was the prototypical high school athlete, tall, dark hair, perfect jaw bone, muscular build and a hit with all the ladies. He was also a bit of a bully. In passing he would always bump my shoulder and stare at me with a "I'm going to kick your ass" look in his eyes.

One day he was having a conversation in the hallway with his girlfriend, Amy Hunter. She was undoubtingly the most beautiful girl I had ever seen. I had a crush on her ever since I first laid eyes on her. I had just finished history class and was headed to my locker. Usually when I looked at Amy she never looked back. This particular time she looked back at me, in the middle of her conversation with Brad. It was like she had seen me for the first time. You could almost see the chemistry in the air. Brad was talking and she was looking at me. I was looking back at her not paying attention to where I was going. If I had paid more attention to my surroundings I would've noticed Brad walking up to me. In an instant he punched the living shit out of me. He hit me so hard my head hit the lockers before I fell to the floor. If I wasn't knocked unconscious I'm pretty sure it would've been the worse paid I ever felt, on top of the embarrassment.

When I finally came to, the hallways were empty. No students, no teachers, no one was in sight. Right away I started experiencing

Choice | James Green

the worst headache ever. When I tried to stand up, I felt someone helping me. I turned around to thank whoever it was but there was no one there. I had always felt the figures presence but it never actually touched me. I made my way to the bathroom to get myself together. Looking at myself in the mirror I noticed the whole right side of my face was red and swollen. I was so pissed...all I could think about was revenge. My heart was pounding, hands sweating and my eyes were watery from the tears built up. I splashed some water on my face and gathered my composure. Before I could exit the bathroom I felt a hand rest itself

28

on my shoulder. I knew there would be no one there if I turned around. It gave me the exact comfort that I needed at the time. There were no words, just the feeling that everything was going to be ok. I left and went back to class and finished the rest of the school day. I was able to function enough to do my work but I was still very angry. I sat there, thinking of different things I wanted to do to Brad. They were very disturbing thoughts. That day I stayed a little later after school to work on my project for the science fair. I was attempting to create a remote control flying race car. It was going to be so cool.

When I finished for the day, I headed to my locker to grab my jacket and the rest of my belongings. The hallway felt a little creepy and a bit chillier than normal. There was a feeling of déjà vu but I had no idea what it was. I paid it no mind and proceeded to put my jacket on. Out of my pocket fell an old brown slightly ripped piece of paper. I picked it up to see what it was. It had words written on it from what looked like some kind of red ink. The words were a little too thick to be from an ink pen I thought. "FOR YOU" it said. I looked around wondering if it was some kind of joke. My first thought was to just throw it away but

I decided to keep it. I placed it in my pocket and began my walk home.

During my stroll home, it got a little breezy so I zipped up my jacket. I just so happened to look down while doing so and noticed a piece of paper that resembled the one I found in my pocket. A little hesitant to pick it up but something told me to just do it. Before I could pick it up the wind blew again and so did the paper. Every step I took the wind blew it a little more. I tried walking a little faster to maybe step on it but the faster I walked the faster the wind blew it. Looking down the whole time I didn't notice where I was actually going.

It finally slowed down a little as I arrived at a forest. "Aleister's Woods" a sign said. I had heard about it before but I or no one I knew had ever been inside. "Well, I've already come this far" I told myself. The paper continued to slowly blow down the main trail. After a few yards down it blew off to the side. Reluctant to go off the trail I followed it anyway, thinking to myself I had already come this far, no point of stopping now. The more I walked the more flies I noticed. I hated flies, the creepy woods didn't help the situation either.

When the paper finally stopped I was able to pick it up. I felt a few rain drops and immediately got frustrated. I was probably lost, just went on a high speed chase to catch a piece of paper and to top things off I was about to get rained on. I looked to the sky to see how dark the clouds were, maybe see how much time I had before the rain really came down. What I saw instead...brought me my knees.

I saw Brad, hanging by his neck, swinging from a huge tree limb. His lifeless body was bloody and naked. What I thought were rain drops turned out to be blood,

dripping from his feet. I had no clue what to do

from there, I was horrified. While stepping

back to get a better look at him, I noticed

something carved in his chest. I wiped my eyes

to make sure I was seeing things clearly. In the

middle of his chest there was a star carved. It

reminded me of the starts we drew on paper in

pre school with all the lines going through

them. The tip of the star pointed towards the

bottom. There were words caved on his

abdomen..." FOR YOU". Quickly I reached for

the paper I still had in my pocket. The moment

was so unreal. Who would commit such a

heinous act? I didn't know of or have any friends that would avenge a punch in the face for me. Brad had to be at least 14-15 feet in the air, how did he even get up there? There was no way anyone had climbed that tree. To make matters worse, Brads blood was all over me, it had dripped on my hair, my face and my clothes. I was a walking body of evidence. "What if the police think I did it?" I said to myself. All the students that saw me get punched by Brad, everyone would probably think I killed him for revenge.

I stood there, debating to myself on calling the police or maybe letting someone know near by. The fact that I was going to be a possible suspect killed both of those idea so I ran home as fast as I could. Turned out Aleister's woods was just an alternate route home and I wasn't lost after all.

As soon as I got home I ran straight to the bathroom to wash any blood I had on me off. While standing there, reality started settling in and just broke down. Burying my face in my hands I cried. Probably hadn't cried that hard since I was a small child. There was too much blood on the shirt so instead of trying to wash it I threw it away. Starring at myself in the mirror, I don't know why, but something told me to turn the lights off. I

flicked the switch, but when I looked back in

the mirror, there was the figure…standing

right behind me. I was surprised because for

the first time It didn't look so undefined. I

could tell the figure had wings. They weren't

spread but you could tell they were mounted

on his back. There weren't any eyes but I could

feel us starring at one another. "Did you do

this?" I asked. For a brief moment it just stood

there, but then it disappeared.

CHAPTER 6

It had been about a week since the incident in the woods. I woke up a little late that day due to the lack of sleep I was getting. Nightmare were constantly consuming my nights.

When I arrived at school, everyone in the hallways where hugging each other and crying. I assumed why but I had to pretend that I didn't know what was going on. Some of the football players where wearing T-shirts with pictures of Brad on them. On the graffiti wall in the athletic hallway the walls read "RIP

BRAD, WE MISS YOU". I saw Amy crying.

Her face was buried in the shoulder of her best

friend Melissa. I thought about the day we got

caught starring at each other. It was an

awkward time but I just had to say something

to her. I walked up to her and softly placed my

hand on her shoulder "Are you ok" I asked.

She looked up and grabbed me as if she missed

me. I could feel my shirt becoming wet from

her tears. I know the feeling was wrong, but as

she cried, deep down I was smiling ear to ear.

There I was, holding the girl of my dreams.

After a few minutes I held her by the arms and

looked her in the eye "If you ever need

anything, anyone to talk to..." She nodded

"Thank you Christian" she said. The rest of the

day seemed like a free day. The teachers were

caught up in emotion to teach anything so each

class we just sat and talked amongst one

another. Everyone was so sad...losing Brad

was a big loss to the school. The principles

voice came over the PA system requesting a

moment of silence to remember their star

quarterback. I'm sure my memory of Brad was

a lot different than everyone else's. To most he

was a handsome hero, to me he was just a jock

and a bully. That bully I found hanging dead

from that tree also had the girlfriend that I wanted.

I decided to get back to reading my Bible. It was the only book that I had been reading over the past few weeks. I wanted to know more about Lucifer, the angel that shared the same name as me. There were so many pages I didn't know where to start to look for him. I took my cell phone out and google searched his name. The more I scrolled through the results the more I became disturbed. "Father of lies, the devil". There were horrible images. I suddenly didn't feel proud of my name anymore. Why would my parents name me that? I clicked on different images, while disgusted, curiosity took over. Out of all the terrible images I saw, there was one particular one that made my stomach turn. I saw the upside down pentagram that was carved on Brad's chest. I researched some more. It said it represented the dark side, a pagan symbol. It was a symbol used by "Satanists" people who worshipped the Devil.

This is actually when my obsession began. I just had to no more. My interest in learning about the Bible turned into wanting to know more about Lucifer. Why was he so evil? Had it been him that's been following me my whole life? If so, why me? I looked up videos, anything I could find on him, just to see what I could learn. I think my biggest mistake in all my research was the purchase I made of a book that I thought would tell me everything I needed to know…" Satan's Bible"

The first day I opened the book I felt the figure's presence like never before. It appeared even more defined than the last time I saw it. It was still black but the wings could be seen more clearly. The outline of his hair could be made out as well. It almost reminded me of my hair. The figure stood roughly six feet six inches, which happened to be about six inches taller than I was. Not sure how I became so frightened at the moment, it wasn't like I hadn't seen him a million times.

It didn't speak so I decided to go back to reading my book. I thought maybe a little reading would calm my nerves. After the first page was turned the figure took a step towards me. My jaws vibrated from the chatter of my teeth. I was so scared, yet at the same time just as curious. Not even looking down I turned another page…the figure took another step forward. That familiar breeze that always gave me the chills passed through. Every page I turned, another step was taken. I turned and turned until it stood just inched away from my

chair. I could feel its breath brushing against

my forehead. At that distance I was too afraid

to turn another page. All of a sudden its wings

spread, they were so huge. They were actually

memorizing, so much that I forgot that I was

afraid. The moment my nerves were calm it

bent over…its face transformed in to a goat. It

stood there no more than an inch from my face.

"READ!!!!" it screamed. Another gust of wind

blew and the figure disappeared. I sat there,

shivering and thinking how close I was to

shitting on myself. That comfort I always felt

when he was around was long gone. I was

petrified at the thought of him returning that

night. I starred at the book, tears falling down

my cheek. Sad thing was…I knew I was going

to read it. I was addicted.

CHAPTER 7

The next day in school, I ran into Amy. She had just finished science class. One look at her always took my stress away. The thought of her alone took my mind off the book, Brad, everything. I mustered up as much courage as I could and approached her "Hey Amy, I was just wondering if you weren't too busy maybe one of these days…. we could go on a date or something." At first her face was emotionless. That awkward moment I was afraid to happen was happening. She smiled a little after a moment "Sure Christian, how about we catch that new scary movie that just came out" "Uh yea absolutely, I love scary movies!" I said. I was a horrible liar; I had never been to the movies due to the fact that I had never been on a date.

Our first date was great! We shared a large popcorn and we each had red slushy's. the movie was a little scary so I was able to put my arm around her. It was everything I dreamed of.

After that we started going out on the weekends, then I'd see her a few times a week. We were having the time of our lives, taking trips to the museums, going to different places to eat, I couldn't ask for more.

An itch began to grow for me to get back to my book. Not sure why I was so eager to get back to it. With every encounter I became more terrified, but I kept reading. There was never a feeling of satisfaction, I had to know more and more. It became a craving. Satanism was the only thing I studied, I even stopped reading books from school. I never practiced anything I read, only the thirst to know what and why consumed me. The things that I would come across were so confusing to me at times. One moment I would find something I could relate to the next I would be sick to my stomach. I bought more books on Satanism from any small book store I could find. I didn't want to borrow from the library; didn't want people to judge or know what I was studying. With all the purchases I was making I was running into a small problem...cash flow.

I picked up a job at the local supermarket to fund my obsession. I had a lot on my plate as a teen, school, work, obsession with the Devil...and my new girlfriend Amy. She started visiting me after school to just chill out. She knew the money from our dates was adding up and was becoming too much for a teens salary. There wasn't anything sexual going on, we'd usually rent a movie, eat or do some homework together. We enjoyed each others company. Sometimes we'd just lay there, cuddling, talking about nothing.

One Friday night we decided to rent an old scary movie. We laid there watching it eating microwaved popcorn. I loved being next to her. She slowly looked up at me, our noses basically touched. She poked her lips out signaling me to kiss her. When our lips touched it felt like the entire world disappeared. It was our first real passionate kiss. I was a little nervous, wondering if she

felt what was happening in my pants. Before I

could go in for another kiss a small breeze

passed through the room. My window was

closed so I quickly became afraid. I looked up

desperately hoping the figure wasn't around. I

checked the corner, the door, even behind me.

"What's wrong babe? Amy asked. I turned

back around to let her know it was nothing

and there the figure was…standing by the bed

behind her. My body went into shock; no

words were able to leave my lips. The figure

never appeared while anyone else was around.

"What is it? Amy asked. I could tell she was a

little scared by the way she was looking. As

she looked in my eyes she could tell I was

looking at something behind her. She quickly

turned around and the figure vanished. "That

movie really got to you huh" she laughed.

"Yea" I responded. I tried to laugh along with

her, she had to know I was faking.

CHAPTER 8

The next morning there was a knock on my door. I turned over to see if Amy was still there. She must've left after I fell asleep, there was a note on my pillow. Before I could open it there was another knock at the door. I opened the door and it was my neighbor, well the kid that stayed in the next bedroom. He reached out his hand "Hey, Mark" he said. I looked down at his hand for a second. All the time we lived under the same roof and this was the first time he ever said more than hello. "Christian" I said as I shook his hand. "So what can I do for you?" I asked. "Actually I've been wanting to meet you for a while, us being neighbors and all. Every time I think about speaking, there's always some um...don't want to be rude, but some kind of creepiness going on with you. Sometimes it seems like you're sad or down about something. I always tell myself, I'll just catch him next time when it looks like he's in a better mood" he laughed. "Yesterday I saw you with a girl and you were finally smiling. I didn't want to interrupt so I figured I'd wait until now so.... here I am!"

I invited Mark in my room. He looked amazed at the things I had. Since I had a job I could afford newer things, a flat screen TV,

dvd player, I also had a nice wireless Bluetooth

player for my music. I sat on the edge of my

bed and he sat on my chair. "I have to be

honest with you" he said. "I also walked to

know, well I hear you talking all the time

through the wall. I never hear anything talking

back. I hear you say hello and good bye but I

never hear anyone come or go."

"You must've heard me speaking to Amy,

she's my girlfriend" I responded.

"No no, I have been hearing you for quite

some time now. I was just curious" he said. I

knew what he was referring to but I played

clueless and said that it must've been the TV or

something. He looked at me strangely, right

away he knew I wasn't that good of a liar.

"Forget I asked" he said. "Anyway, do you

want to hang out sometime? We can go to the

mall, eat or hang out at the malt shop." Wow! I

thought, my first friend! "Sure man" I told

Mark. "Ok cool, well I guess I'll see you

around then" he smiled and went back to his

room.

CHAPTER 9

I reached for the note Amy had left for me...

"Sorry I didn't wake you before I left, you were fast asleep and I didn't want to wake you,

Love, Amy xoxo"

That was the first time anyone used the word love in regards to me. Smiling from ear to ear I placed the note inside my nightstand, next to it was a picture of Amy and I, a selfie she took of us while walking through the park one day. There was something different about the picture; when I picked it up I noticed Amy's face had been burned. Who would do such a thing? Thinking about what happened to Brad I quickly panicked and quickly grabbed my phone to call Amy.

"Hello…hello! Hello? Are you ok?" breathing heavily waiting on a response.

She laughed "Yes honey, why wouldn't I be? You're not still creeped out by that movie are you?"

"Yea, yea I must be" I said before hanging up. I was so relieved that I forgot my manners, Amy didn't get a chance to say ok or goodbye or anything.

I decided to take a short nap before getting back to my book. A little skeptical to read it wondering if the figure was upset with me.

About an hour later I woke up in a cold sweat. It was the most horrific nightmare. I had to be about three years old; I woke up from the smell of smoke and a breeze that gave me the chills. I ran to my bedroom door to escape. When I opened it, everything was on fire. I could hear my mom coughing, crying, screaming my name. I saw my dad running out of the front door. For some reason I couldn't get a good look at him. I made an attempt to go to my mother. It only took about

two steps before the floor caved in and I saw

her fall through the floor along with other

burning parts of the house. I tried to run down

the stairs to save her but someone quickly

picked me up and rushed my outside. It

must've been a fireman because I could feel his

hard helmet tapping against my head as he

ran. We stood in the yard, far from the house

watching the rest of the firemen take on the

fire, holding hands. I looked up to see the face

of the man that saved my life. When he looked

down at me his face suddenly transformed into

the face of a goat, the same goat the figure's

face changed to before..." READ!" it yelled. I

let out the most terrifying scream while quickly

waking up. My bed was soaked with sweat;

my heart was pounding...it was hard to go to

sleep after that.

CHAPTER 10

When I finally was able to calm down, I picked up my book and began reading. The words were there but I wasn't comprehending anything. Thoughts of my mom, watching her die kept replaying in my mind. I had only known her for three years of my life but I missed her so much. The urge to know what really happened took over me. I wanted to know about my dad. Who was he? What did he look like? And why didn't he try to help us?

Realizing I was almost late for work, I hopped up and changed clothes. I arrived at work just in time for my shift to start. I didn't speak to anyone or let anyone know I was there, Immediately I just started stocking the shelves.

A little later into my shift I noticed I still hadn't seen anyone. I preferred being out of the way but it wasn't normal to not see my manager at least once. The boxes that needed to be stocked seemed endless. Everything was quiet, a little too quiet. Looking around I noticed there weren't any customers, no employees, things were getting a little too creepy. I walked towards the front of the store, still no one. Suddenly there was a tap on my shoulder. When I turned around it was an old lady standing there. "Excuse me" she said "Can you tell me where my daughter is?"

"What?" I responded. I had no clue what she was talking about. "Can you tell me where my daughter is, I can't find her" she said again. I didn't know what to do so I grabbed the old lady by the hand and walked her towards the security desk. "Did you lose her in here?" I asked. "No" she said" She died in a house fire in 1985...AND YOU'RE NEXT!" When I turned to look at her, her face had transformed into that hideous goat that I saw in my nightmare. I threw her hand down and ran as fast as I could. I could hear her creepy laugh as I ran out of the store. What was happening to me? Ever since I got punched in the face it seemed like my life was taking a turn for the worse.

I needed to take my mind off things somehow so I immediately started to think about Amy. I began daydreaming about her cute little smile and the way she tossed her hair before she spoke. I was so deep in thought I began drifting in the street. Suddenly there was a loud horn and the sound of screeching breaks as a green Honda Civic slammed into me. I rolled on top of the hood, I remember the sound of the windshield cracking. Before

rolling over the entire car, I felt myself being

picked up. When the car passed I was gently

placed on the ground without a scratch. The

man driving the car franticly ran towards me.

"HEY ASSHOLE!" he said gripping me by the

shoulders. It was a middle aged man, bald at

the top, slicked down black hair on the sides.

"WHAT WERE YOU THINKING HUH?!" he

yelled while shaking me. "I'm ok" I responded.

He pushed me away and headed towards his

car "BE MORE FUCKING CAREFUL NEXT

TIME, DUMBASS" I was still in shock from the

whole ordeal that I didn't pay him much

attention. As I turned around to head home I heard a huge explosion! BOOOOM!! The force of the blast pushed me to the ground. The Honda civic was up in flames, along with the rude middle aged man. Again, panicked, I ran home as fast as my feet could carry me.

When I got home I pushed the front door open and ran up stairs. Mark was on his way out "Hey Christian" he said as I blew by him, I didn't stop to speak, I needed to get to my room. I slammed my door shut and plopped down in my chair, face buried in my hands. I was so confused, so scared. I heard my door opening "Hey you ok dude?" Mark asked as he stood in the doorway. I didn't have the energy to speak so I shook my head no. He placed his hand on my shoulder before sitting on the edge of my bed. "What's your story" he asked.

My first thought was to say none of his business but I was actually pretty flattered that he actually cared to ask. I took a deep breath, looked him in the eye and began to tell him my story. I told him about the fire, the little I knew about my father. I told him about the few memories I had of my mom. It felt like I was having a session with a psychiatrist. I did though, leave out a small detail about my life.

There was no way I was going to tell him about the figure. I didn't want to lose the only friend I had that quickly. He seemed pretty interested in what I was talking about; I could tell he knew I was holding something back.

"I know a lady, well I've heard of a lady" Mark said. "I hear she can talk to spirits…you know, dead people." "Dead people?" I responded. "Yea, you know, maybe she can contact your mom" said Mark. As crazy as it sounded, I was intrigued. How the hell was she going to do that? was the first thing that crossed my mind. It didn't matter, I knew I was going the moment Mark

mentioned it.

"OK" I said "I'll go." "Ok man, I'll see

what I can do, maybe set something up." Mark

got up and closed the door behind him.

CHAPTER 11

I noticed some writing on the door after Mark shut it. "LOSE HER" it said. It looked like it was written in red paint. I got up to get a closer look, wondering how it even got there. Rubbing my finger through the letters I instantly knew it was blood. It was the same way Brad's blood looked on my hands. A small breeze passed through my room. Goose bumps began to form on my arms. Behind me I heard pages flapping. When I turned around I saw my book was open and laying in the middle of my bed. Out of curiosity, I picked it up and began reading. There was a light coming from

my nightstand. It crept through the cracks of

the drawer. When I opened it I saw my Holy

Bible sitting on top of everything. It was on top

of my pictures, even the letter I got from Amy.

I didn't remember sitting it on top like that. I

paid it no mind and closed the drawer.

I went back to reading my Satanic Bible.

The subject I was reading at the time talked

about sacrifice. It went into grave detail about

sacrificing animals, small children and young

women. It also mentioned the benefits of what

you would gain if you participated in such

acts. Some of the things I read were very

disturbing. I couldn't understand why things like that would come with a reward.

"Christian..." I heard a voice but I couldn't tell where it was coming from. I got up and checked the closet, under the bed, but there was nothing. When I stood up the figure was right there, standing directly in front of me. It startled me so much I fell back in my chair. "Christian..." it said in a calm voice. I could finally tell that the figure was for sure a man. "Christian..." it repeated. "Yes" I responded, I could feel the chatter of my teeth. With the deepest, darkest, loudest, most terrifying voice I had ever heard "LOSE HER!"

it screamed before flying out of the window. It was then I realized that it was the figure that murdered Brad; it was him that burned a hole in my picture with Amy. It was him that wrote on my door with God know whose blood. I thought about the car explosion and the rude old man. I sat there wondering if he had anything to do with that missing kid all those years ago. If he was supposed to be protecting me, why would want me to get rid of my first and only girlfriend? Amy was the best thing that ever happened to me. I was flattered by the protection but by no means did I want anyone to die. There wasn't a chance in hell I was going to dump Amy...but what would he

do if I didn't?

CHAPTER 12

About a week or so went by and everything seemed to be going back to normal. I would read and the figure would be there just standing in the corner, almost as if he were pleased. I tried my best to avoid Amy until I figured things out. I would tell her that I was busy with work or school or that Mark and I had plans to hang out.

It was an early Saturday morning, I was awaken by an alert from my cell phone. I reached for the floor where I usually kept it but it wasn't there. I checked under my pillows, the pants I had worn the previous day but I still couldn't find it. It beeped again; I followed the sound and it led me to my nightstand. I opened the drawer and saw that my phone was sitting on top of my Holy Bible. I knew for sure that I didn't put my phone there. How did it get there? The caller ID read that I had a missed call from Amy. Before I could return her call, Amy had called again. It startled me a little but I was happy to see her name again. I answered..." Christian" she said. I could tell she had been crying by the tone of her voice. "What's wrong?" I asked.

"What's going on with you? Why does it seem like things are different between us? Did I do something wrong?"

I knew it was my fault and that I was hurting her. I didn't want to break up with her but I didn't want put her life at risk either. "I just have a lot going on Amy" I said. "WELL TELL ME!" she yelled.

Honestly I didn't know what to say. I began telling her about my parents and the house fire that happened when I was a child. I told her about the fireman, the paramedics and how I ended up in the orphanage. I left out any parts regarding the haunting figure of course.

Too afraid of how she would react, I never mentioned it.

"Hey Amy" I said interrupting her "Do you believe in the Devil? I could tell the question threw her off a little. "Like the guy in red with the horns and the pitch fork?" she asked. "I guess" I said. "I mean I never really thought about it" she answered.

I took a moment and decided I was going to tell her about the figure. I knew I loved her with all my heart and knew that she loved me. Eventually I was going to have to tell her anyway. "I have to tell you something Amy" I said.

"Yes Christian"

"I…"

"CHRISTIAN, CHRISTIAN!" Mark burst in my room before I could finish what I was saying. "I got good news buddy"

"Christian, what is it?" Amy said. I couldn't tell her with Mark in the room so I told her I would call her back later that day. She sounded a little disappointed but hung up without a fight. "Well" Mark said "Remember I told you about the woman that could talk to dead people, I got us a meeting!"

Mark was really excited about the whole thing. I wondered if he had anyone he wanted to speak to. I myself, had a million

questions I wanted to ask my mom. Extremely

nervous, but I was really anxious to get there

and talk to the lady. "So when is the meeting?"

I asked. He had a funny look on his face,

almost as if he didn't want to tell me…" In

about 4 hours" he said. "FOUR HOURS!" I

didn't expect a meeting anytime soon but

realizing I literally had nothing else to do I

agreed to go.

The appointment was at the woman's

house. Madam Blavatsky was her name. her

house was about a thirty-minute walk away.

The weather was nice and enjoyed spending

time with Mark. We laughed and joked around wondering what the lady might say when we asked her questions. Deep down I missed Amy so much, but It was nice having a guy friend.

"Man, that is one big ass bird" Mark said. I looked up and saw a flock of black birds all flying in the same direction. "Which one?" I asked. He pointed to the bird in front of the flock. "That's no bird" I whispered to myself. I never saw the figure in the daylight but I had seen him enough to know that it was him. The huge wings looked all too familiar. I didn't want Mark to know how scared I had just become. "What?" he asked. "Yea yea, that is a big bird" I said attempting to look normal.

The flock of birds were flying in the same direction as we were. If we made a turn, so did they. Mark found it very strange.

When we reached Madam Blavatsky's house, the birds flew away. The house was amazing! It was so huge, Mark and I had never seen a house like that before.

CHAPTER 13

We arrived at the front door and just stood there, staring at each other. Mark was as creeped out as I was. Before either of us could knock the door opened. There was no one there to greet us, it seemed too much like a scary movie for my liking. "Lets get out of here" I said to Mark. He agreed and we turned around to leave. Suddenly we heard a pleasant voice with a German accent. "Mark, Christian so glad you could make it" it was a beautiful lady in her mid 30's. She wore a scarf around her head just like a fortuneteller. "Come come, we have much to do" she said as she led us to her basement.

To my surprise there were other people waiting. There were five waiting tables placed around the main table where Madam Blavatsky did her work. Each table had a game in the middle, to kill time I imagine. The first table had dominoes, the next one had a pair of dice in the middle. There was another table that had an Ouija board, the next a chess board and the last one had Mexican Bingo (that was the first time I had ever seen or heard of that game)

There were two seats for Mark and I at the Ouija board table. All the games seemed so random. There were red candles lit throughout the entire basement. One of the walls had a beautiful angels painted on it. I had never seen anything like it. The ceiling was painted like a night sky, there were stars everywhere. Some of the stars formed different constellations. In the middle was a huge sun that was directly over the table that Madam Blavatsky sat. I didn't understand how there was a sun in a night sky but either way it was a nice painting.

Madam B. stood up from her seat, it was time to begin…" Everyone, it is time, you will all be helped in the order that you came. First up, may I see Ms. Laura Hamilton." A woman stood up at the table that had the chess board on it. She walked over to the main table and sat across from Madam B. "What is it that I may do for you my dear" she asked. "Laura looked around the room for a second, she seemed to be a bit nervous. "I want to speak to my dead grandmother" she said.

Madam B. closed her eyes. After a few moments, her eyes began to roll until you could only see the whites of her eyes. She started convulsing, I wasn't sure if I was supposed to see if she was ok or just sit there. I started to get up to help and then her eyes

opened. "Your grandmother says she would

love to speak to you Laura, are you ready?"

When Laura agreed, a familiar gust of wind

blew throughout the basement. All the candles

blew out except for the ones that surrounded

the main table. Madam B. closed her eyes again

and lowered her head. "She is ready" she said

softly. I looked over at Mark, he was paralyzed

in fear.

"Hey, you ok? You don't believe any of

this shit do you?" I whispered. He lifted his

hand slowly and pointed to the wall across the

room. There was a light slowly coming

through the wall. "Laura...Laura...this is your grandmother" a voice said. The voice seemed to be coming from the light. Laura was so terrified that she couldn't muster up any words. When the light finally made its way through completely, we could see the image of an old woman.

"WOW!" Mark...do you see" before I could finish Mark was already running towards the door. There was no way I was going to stay down there alone so I ran after him. I kept calling his name as I chased him down the street. Mark was either extremely scared or extremely fast. It took a minute for me to catch up with him. By the time I caught him we were both out of breath.

"Christian" he said. It was hard for him to get his words out. "Dude, I'm sorry, I didn't know it was going to be like that, I thought it was going to be some creepy old lady that read some tarot cards to us and we paid her a dollar or something. What the hell was that we just saw?" I was bent over, holding my knees still trying to catch my breath. "I don't know man" I said. I knew what we saw was crazy, but honestly I was amazed. I kept thinking how was it even possible? As we walked home I wondered did Laura learn anything about her grandmother. I wondered what would've

happened when it was my turn…would any of

my questions have been answered? Not

wanting to get Mark any more worked up, I

kept my thoughts to myself.

CHAPTER 14

A few days had gone by since the visit

to Madam B's house. Mark was still a bit

shaken up but he never said anything about it.

The figure still came to visit every night. I

would read and it would stand in the

corner...things were normal again. I wondered

if he forgot about Amy. I wanted to see her so

bad. Prom was coming up soon so I decided to

give her a call. To my surprise, she was happy

to hear from me.

"Christian, I have something I want to

talk to you about" she said. I didn't let her

finish; I was too excited to talk about prom.

"Just promise me one thing" she said "Promise me we don't have to wear black" I laughed and happily agreed.

Back at school, you could tell everyone had prom on the mind. Everyone was discussing what to wear or what kind of car they were going to drive. After my math class, I walked the halls looking for Amy. I bumped shoulders with a student that I had never seen before. She was wearing a nice pair of black eyeglasses, a white button up shirt and a pair of light blue jeans. She dressed very conservative.

"Excuse me, I'm sorry" I said to her.

"Hello Christian" she said. I was a little

confused and pretty much speechless, how did

she know my name? "Are you interested in

knowing the truth?" she asked. I didn't know

how to respond, I had no idea what the hell

she was talking about. "Do you know who

Jesus Christ is?" she added. The moment felt

too awkward at that point so I slowly started to

walk away. "Do not give place to the Devil

Christian!" she hollered as I faded away into

the crowd. No one in the hallway seemed to

even notice her. The bell rang and the hallways

were instantly empty. I missed seeing Amy

with all the time I spent listening to the strange

girl.

I met up with Amy after school to go

pick out a dress for her and a tuxedo for me to

wear to prom. The employee was very helpful

with helping us pick out what to wear. She

handed Amy a beautiful white dress to go try

on in the dressing room. While she was

changing, I wanted to ask the lady her opinion

on the tux I had picked out. As I was speaking

to her, her face slowly went from a nice smile,

to a serious frown…she almost looked

possessed. "LOSE HER" she said. Her voice

sounded the exact same as the figure's. "I'm

sorry?" I replied. "LOSE HER!!!" she said again in the same voice.

Amy came from behind the dressing room door and the woman's face quickly changed back to the pretty smile she had prior. I didn't say anything; I didn't want to startle Amy. When she decided on the dress I quickly reserved it and left the store. I was so much in a rush that I forgot to reserve the tux for myself. When Amy noticed she reminded me but I told that I didn't see anything that I liked and would pick one out another day, maybe even from different place.

When we arrived back at my place,

there was an envelope slid under my door.

"Who's that from?" Amy asked. There was no

return address on the envelope, it only had my

name written on it in red ink. I was afraid to

open it, but to keep Amy from being

suspicious, I opened it anyway. It was an

invitation…it also had Mark's name on it. It

was an invitation to meet with Madam B again.

The date was set for the upcoming Sunday.

"DO NOT MISS" it read at the bottom. I ran

next door to show Mark.

"No fucking way dude, how did she

even get our address?" I actually wondered the

same thing. Either way, I had to go back. There

were too many questions I needed answers to.

I started to wonder why the figure was so close

by when we were walking to Madam B's

house. Was he trying to lead us there?

When I got back to my room, I saw Amy

holding a book in her hand. I hurried up and

took it from her. There was no way she was

going to know I was reading the Satanic Bible.

To my surprise the book I snatched from her

hands was my Holy Bible. "I didn't know you

read the Bible" she said. She seemed so

pleased. "Um, yea, I started it but I never

finished…have you read it? I asked. "Well,

actually I just started since you asked me about the Devil. I figured I might as well not go the rest of my life not knowing anything you know?" she smiled. "What made you look in my night a stand?" I asked. "It was just laying here on the pillow" she said. That must've been the 2nd time the Bible moved without me touching it. I knew couldn't have been going crazy. Right away, I wondered where my other book was. I scanned the room trying to not let her see that I was actually looking for something. It was laying on the floor next to the bed. I gently slid it under the bed with my foot. It was a close call but I really wasn't ready to tell her about what I had been doing in my spare time. "Oh, Christian I almost forgot, I really have to talk to you about something" she reminded me. "Can it wait?" I asked. I was so exhausted. She didn't want to, reluctantly she said ok.

Choice | James Green

CHAPTER 15

Surprisingly, that Sunday I convinced

Mark to go back to Madam B's house with me.

I had no intentions of missing our appointment

whether or not Mark chose to go. The "DO

NOT MISS" on the invitation spoke enough

volume for me alone...Mark had no idea what

the figure was capable of and I didn't want

him to experience it.

We began our journey to Madam

Blavatsky's, the walk was a lot quieter than the

last. "Hey, I meant to tell you I had Death

tickets next week, you want to go? Mark asked.

Death was a popular rock band that actually came from our city. It was their first time returning home since they became famous and starting doing music videos and going on world tours and things like that. "Hell yea I want to go!" I said. The excitement over the bad helped distract us from how we were actually feeling. I kept looking to the sky, looking for the flock of black birds we saw before. We didn't see them until we arrived at Madam B's house. They were hovering over her house, flying in circles. There was one that wasn't flying, it sat there parked on the edge of the roof. It felt like it was watching us. "Dude what kind of bird is that? I mean I've seen huge birds, but never one that big, it almost looks like a person doesn't it? Mark said. "I don't know man, maybe it's a big vulture." I replied. "Yea, maybe" he said as we reached the front door.

I reached to ring the doorbell but before I could Mark pushed the front door open. We looked at each other, simultaneously took a deep breath and headed towards the basement. I was ok at first, but Mark was so nervous it began to rub off on me. "Hello boys" Madam B said as she met us at the bottom of the stairs. "I'm sorry I did not come up and let you in but

I was talking to the spirit and couldn't break contact. But I see you both found your way, good, please sit."

We sat and waited, same table, same as as the last time. Mark whispered "Dude do you think these Ouija boards really work?" I've seen them on TV but I always wondered if the people were faking." I looked at the board. It wasn't too much to it, there were some letters, numbers and a triangular looking piece with a magnifying glass in the middle. "Only one way to find out" I replied.

We both put our hands on the triangular piece and looked at each other. "Dude, ask it a question" Mark was anxious to try it out. "I don't know what to ask it" I said. I looked around the room trying to come up with a question. There was a young woman sitting across from us at the table with the chess board. She was pretty, she had blonde hair and green eyes. She had on red high heels and a black mini skirt. She smiled at me when she noticed I was looking at her. She nodded then went back to playing chess. Madam B was at the main table lighting the rest of the candles. She took a seat and closed her eyes. There was no movement, no words, she just sat there.

"Dude, hurry up and ask it a question!" Mark said in a loud whisper. "Um dear Ouija board, please tell us, something Ummmm important!" I had no idea what to ask, pretty sure what I said wasn't even a question.

"What" Mark said looking at me like was in idiot. "Dude what d" before Mark finished our hands began to move. The piece seemed to be moving to different letters. "Dude you're moving it!" Mark laughed. I could tell by the way he said it that it wasn't him moving it either. I raised my head to see the letters it was hovering over. E,P,H,E,S,I there was a pen and paper on the table so I had to remember what the letters were so I could write them down. It

kept going...A,N,S,4,2,7. When it stopped

moving I quickly grabbed the pen and wrote

down the letters. EPHESIANS427 was what I

had written down. Mark grabbed the pad.

"EPHESIANS 427? What the hell is that? it

sounds like a bible verse" Mark said. It

sounded familiar but I couldn't remember if I

read anything in the Bible with that title.

"Put your hands back on" Mark said. I

could tell he was getting impatient. "Dude,

you have to ask it something specific,

something crazy, like this.... Dear Ouija board,

who is the next person that is going to die!"

our hands began to move again. Mark sat back

and waited to see what I was going to write.

The first letter it hovered over was M, and then

it slowly moved to the A. it was moving

towards the next letter…" Christian, Mark, I

am ready now" Madam B said. She called us

before I got to see the rest of the letters. "So

what did it say?" Mark asked. "I don't know,

she called us before I could see the rest of it" I

replied.

He put his hand on my shoulder on the

way to the main table. "Hope it wasn't going to

say me" he said smiling. Madam B looked at

us, batting her eyes and smiling "Now which

one of you would like to go first?" Mark

pointed at me. "I would like to speak to my

mother" I said. She nodded "very well"

She closed her eyes as a deep silence

took over the room. It almost looked like she

fell asleep. I thought about tapping her to

make sure but a few seconds later, a familiar

breeze entered the room. The flames in the

candles blew as it entered. There were voices,

whispering all around us, but we couldn't see

where they were coming from. Cracks in the

wall began to form with bright lights shining

through them. More and more light came

through the cracks, something was trying to
come in.

"Christian" I heard a voice whisper
from the wall. I looked over to Madam B, her
head was still down and here eyes were closed.
I looked to Mark, his eyes were also closed and
he was shivering uncontrollably. The voice
called me again as the light slowly crept
through the cracks.

When the light finally made its way
through it was too bright to look at. As the rays
died down I saw a woman. She hovered in the
air like a ghost in the movies. As I adjusted my
eyes I was able to focus on the woman's

face…it was my mother! She appeared to be sad and still had that running mascara on her cheeks that I always dreamed about. "I love you son" she said. Her lips didn't move but her voice was as clear as day. All the questions I had for her and at the moment couldn't think of one. She spoke again "The girl, you must…." She started fading back into the wall. "MOM WAIT! WHAT GIRL?" I yelled. In an instant, her, along with the light had faded away. The wall looked as if nothing ever happened, no light no cracks. My sight became blurry from the tears that were trying to form. It was the first time I had seen my mother since

I was a child. Madam B didn't wake up right away. The blonde haired woman gathered her things and made her way towards the stairs. For some reason I could feel her looking at me before she walked out the door. Mark's eyes were still closed "Is it over?" he asked. "I saw my mom" I said. I burst into tears, it was too much to hold in.

Madam B woke up…" Next, Tom Jennings please." I stood up and tapped Mark on the shoulder "Lets go". As we walked up the stairs Madam B said her farewell "I will see you boys soon." I planned on leaving her house with clarity, some closure about my life.

All I left with was more confusion and the

need to know more. I started to wonder about

the house my mom died in. Was it still

standing? I had no idea where it was...I

decided to make that my next project.

CHAPTER 16

It was the day of the Death concert. It was my first time going to a concert so I was pretty excited. I wanted Amy to go with us but Mark could only score us two tickets. As I was getting dressed an alert sounded from my phone. It was a text message from Amy *"Hey Christian, just wanted to tell you to have fun and be safe at the concert. Please text me when you get back."* Curiosity was eating me at that point; what was it she wanted to tell me so badly? I sent her a message back…*" What is it you wanted to talk to me about?"* She didn't respond right away so I continued getting dressed. By the time I finished she responded *"I don't want to tell you over text, I will talk to you about it when I see you."* I was a little confused and slightly annoyed but I didn't make a big deal about it. Mark was still getting dressed so I decided to read a little while I waited. Reaching for my book on my night stand I noticed my Holy Bible was sitting right next to my Satanic Bible. How did my books keep moving? My Holy Bible was on the lamp, in the middle was my lamp and to the right was my Satanic Bible. The light seemed to be shining more on my Holy Bible. I picked it up and placed it back inside my drawer. I had all intentions of getting back to it someday, its just that my obsession wouldn't allow me to read anything else.

As I opened the book I felt something reach over me and open the book for me. The section it opened to the subject was "Invitation". It stated that one could only join a sect through invitation only. I sat there wondering was someone going to show up at my door with a black robe and a bloody invitation in their hand inviting me to some cult. Laughing at the thought, I went back to my reading. My door flew open and it was

Mark standing there, ready to go. "Dude, are you rea…" the door quickly slammed in Mark's face. I ran to the door to see if he was ok. He was holding his nose with blood profusely leaking out. "What the hell man, what did you do to the door!" I didn't respond and just led him to the bathroom so he could clean himself up.

"Do you want to go the hospital and get it checked out?" I asked. His nose was red and a little swollen. "Dude, I wouldn't miss this concert if that door took my fucking nose off. This is Death we are talking about here." I

laughed and nudged him on the shoulder "Ok
tough guy, lets go."

We caught a cab to the arena. Everyone
was dressed so crazy. People had their face
painted, some wore wigs, some people wore
big black wings. There were a few fans
carrying around pitch forks and making noises
that honestly I couldn't describe if I tried. The
smell of alcohol and sweat dwelled in the air.
Our tickets were close to the front, right in the
middle of the madness.

When the show finally began, all the
lights shut off. The leader of the band, Jethro
Baine, appeared in the middle of the stage with

a huge spotlight shining on him. The crowd went wild. Cheering and screaming along with the crowd I couldn't help but notice what he was doing. As I focused in on him, I noticed he was praying. He looked up and gave a loud scream! There were fireworks shooting up from then the band appeared behind him. Behind the band there was a large screen. It had the image of a black pyramid on it. The band started playing and the crowd went into a frenzy. Mark and I played air guitar, pretending we knew the words to the songs.

During the sixth song, Jethro began running around the stage. He stopped in the middle and looked out into the crowd. Out of

the thousands of people there it seemed like he

was looking directly at me. He pointed his

finger at me as he was finishing the verse. He

sang the words "Yooooou willlll seeee". I'm

pretty sure I was the only one that thought it

was strange. My eyes wandered to the top of

the large screen. I couldn't believe my eyes. It

was the figure, sitting there…sitting there as if

he was enjoying the show. His humungous

wings spread as we looked at each other.

"What the hell are you doing here" I

whispered to myself. Mark was so into the

show that he didn't notice. I pretended as if

everything was normal and just hoped that no one was going to be hurt.

When the show was over, Mark and I were exhausted. All the jumping around and playing air guitar took all of our energy. We waited in front of the arena for our ab to pick us up. A large Mercedes van pulled up in front of us. It looked super expensive. The back window rolled down, I had never seen anything like it before.

"Hey you two, come here" a guy with an English accent called out to us. We ran up to the van to see who it was…it was Jethro! He asked us what were were doing for the rest of the night. We tried to sound important naming random things but we actually had absolutely nothing to do. "Why don't you boys come grab a bite to eat with me, my treat" he implied. The moment was so unreal, quickly we jumped in the van. We were expecting to see the rest of the band but it was just Jethro.

"Hey boys" a female voice came from the front seat. I turned around to see who it was and it was the blonde haired woman we saw at Madam B's house. "Fellas, this is my lovely wife, Diana" Jethro said. I could tell by his grin he was madly in love. For the rest of the ride we didn't say much. Jethro was on his call phone and Mark played with the CD

player they had in the back seat.

We pulled up to a huge, amazing

restaurant. It looked like a castle with

spotlights shining all around it. There were

expensive cars parked in the front. People had

on nice suits and tuxedos. Mark and I still had

on our clothes that we wore to the concert, tees

and jeans. "Aren't we a little underdressed to

get in?" I asked Jethro. "No worries man,

you're with me" he said as we climbed out of

the van. The instant Jethro's foot touched the

ground there were camera flashing and people

with recorders asking questions. It was a bit

too much for me. I knew then that I never

wanted to be famous. Rich maybe, but famous,

not a chance. When we reached the front

entrance we were greeted by a guy in a black

tux. He had a white cloth hanging over his

forearm. "Good evening Mr. Jethro, your table

awaits you" He sat us at a table that easily

could've fit ten people, but it was only the four

of us Mark and I sat directly across from Jethro

and his wife. She was so beautiful; she almost

gave me the same butterflies Amy gave me

when I looked at her. Thinking about what

happened last time I stared at another man's

woman I quickly looked down at my menu.

"So boys, my wife tells me you guys are regulars at the spiritual council meetings." He laughed a little and leaned forward "You guys don't believe in that stuff do you, like you're really talking to the dead" "I don't understand" I responded. Jethro looked at his wife and smiled. "Never mind that, my wife likes to go here and there, it makes her feel good, she thinks it helps people, you know give them a sense of peace. So tell me, do you like stuff like this?" He looked up at the ceiling then pointed to a guy coming in being escorted by two beautiful women. "The money, the toys, the women and all that stuff" he asked.

Mark and I looked at each other as if he asked us the dumbest question in the world. "Yes" we said at the same time.

Jethro nodded and added "Let me ask you guys, how do you guys think I got all of this, the money, the fame…" "Hard work, dedication maybe a little bit of good luck" I replied. "Being a good singer" Mark added. Jethro laughed so hard at our responses that tears came from his eyes. "A good singer he says, its Mark right? Listen to me…I can't sing worth shit. No one, and I mean no one gets anywhere in the world without a higher power working for them" There was a brief silence.

"You mean like God?" I asked. Jethro laughed again. "Like God" he said mocking me "I've been sent here to meet you guys and invite you to a meeting. I'd gladly take you but I'll be on tour so you'll have to find your own way there" He wrote down an address on a napkin and slid it to me.

"How did you find us?" I asked. He told us that he was led to us and that he knew where we were going to be. He even knew where we were during the show. Maybe he really was looking at me when he pointed during that song. Mark was really impressed by all the money, women and power. He had a huge smile on his face the entire time we were there.

When our food arrived, it was brought out by four different waiters. There were steaks, shrimp, bread, a huge salad, sushi, cab legs, lobster, and a few other things I had never seen before. We ate and had small talk the rest of the time there. When the bill came the waiter slid it past me and I happened to see the total. Two thousand dollars! Jethro pulled out a huge wad of cash and threw it on the table. "Alright boys, let's go" We met the van at the front entrance. We hopped in and he took us back home. We thanked him for the ride and exited the van. He called out to us before he pulled off "Don't forget the meeting boys" he waved and threw us a wad of cash as the van pulled off. It must have been somewhere around five thousand dollars. We were in high school so that kind of money had us feeling like we had just hit the lottery. My first thought was to quit my job. Next, I wanted to buy something nice for Amy, maybe something she could show off at prom.

I was able to get a nicer tux since I didn't have to work with a minimum wage budget. While we were walking back to our rooms, I wondered if we went to the meeting, would there be more cash? I always dreamed

of driving a red Ferrari and with that kind of

money it was all possible! I would be the

coolest kid at Lockwood high.

CHAPTER 17

The next day I quit my job. I didn't call
and give a notice, I just assumed they would
notice that I never came back. I remembered
my measurements from the tuxedo rental place
so I ordered a suite for prom from this website
that sold expensive suits. I ordered a pair of
expensive shoes and a nice belt. I sat at my
computer trying to think of things I could
order, things that I couldn't afford before.

Before I got carried away I remembered
I wanted to get Amy something nice. I had no
clue what to get her so I plotted on a way to

probe her for information to see what she
liked.

The next day at school, everyone could
tell I had a different walk. Having money in
my pocket gave me a different kind of
confidence. Most of it I kept in my pocket so
much so that you could see a bulge in my
thigh.

I ran into Amy in the hallway "Hey
baby" I said as I leaned on the locker next to
her. She looked at me strangely "What's gotten
into you" she said giggling. I told her that I
missed her and asked her what she wanted to
talk to me about. She paused for a moment and

told me that it wasn't a good time to talk about it. I was a little concerned and even more curious. I changed the subject and told her that I ordered my suit for prom. I didn't tell her about the Rolls Royce I rented for us; thought it would be a cool surprise.

"So…what would be the perfect gift for the perfect girl?" I asked. Not being a great actor, she could tell what I was implying. "I don't want anything, as long as I have you" she said touching my cheek. "Oh yea, guess what! You'll never believe what happened to me and Mark" I told her about the Death concert, how we met Jethro and the dinner he took us to. I didn't mention the money he gave us and the meeting we were supposed to attend. I hated keeping secrets from her but I wanted to keep her protected, she was all I had. I planned on telling her everything one day, just wasn't sure when exactly. It was a good thing she wasn't too pressed about receiving a gift, after all my spending my money was getting a little low. I had quit my job so I needed a way to make some more money. I wondered if I just kept going to meetings could that be the way?

When I returned home, I checked with Mark to see if he was going to the meeting with me. I had money on the brain, I was going regardless of his decision. Mark was just as excited to go as I was and his cash was running a little thin as well. I looked in his room and noticed he bought a new flat screen television, a new gaming system, he also had some new clothes and even a gold watch! "Been spending I see" I laughed. "Well...maybe a little" Mark laughed along.

The meeting was set for that weekend. The place was far so we were going to have to catch a cab to get there. I had no idea what it was going to be like I wondered if there was going to be a bunch of rock stars there, maybe I would see a few famous people…then it hit

me. I realized what kind of meeting we were

going to. Recalling what I had read regarding

being rewarded for doing things I couldn't

imagine doing. I thought about the money

again and decided to take a chance anyway.

Maybe it wasn't going to be so bad; maybe we

would just go the meeting, they'd give us some

money for attending and we'd be able to leave.

CHAPTER 18

It was Sunday, the day of the meeting. Mark and I were so anxious we woke up hours before it was time to go. All we talked about was what we were going to buy with our next lump sum of money. I told him how eventually I wanted a red Ferrari. Its amazing how many things a kid in high school can think of to buy. I'm sure most of our ideas were dumb, but they sounded genius to us.

The cab picked us up at 10am on the dot and we were on our way. After about an hour of driving I noticed how different everything began to look. The houses were getting larger and the cars were getting more expensive. The streets even looked cleaner. It was about and hour and a half drive before we reached our destination. I wish I could describe how huge the house actually was. If you combined two regular houses, it still wouldn't equal half the size of it. Mark and I split the cab fare since it was so high. I hated the thought of having to pay that again.

As we walked towards the front door we noticed the large fountains that had angels made of stone spitting water from their mouths. The grass was a beautiful shade of green and the bushes were cut to perfection.

There were at least 20 cars parked in front of

the house and they all fit perfectly. Every car

was a Porsche, a Lamborghini, a Rolls Royce,

Mercedes or an Audi…and then I saw my

baby. Some one had a red Ferrari 599 GTB, just

like the one I had been dreaming about every

day. "Come on let's go!" I ran the rest of the

way to the front door.

I rang the doorbell. The butler opened

the door, he had a big mustache. "Hello, may I

help you" he said. I expected him to know who

we were like Madam B did but I was mistaken.

"Um, we were invited by Jethro, you know the

guy from the rock band, he told us to come here today." I don't know why I was so nervous. The butler looked us up and down and pulled a list out of his pocket. "Mark and Christian" I said as he scanned the list. We stood there, awkwardly waiting.

"Maybe we have the wrong place" I tapped Mark and began to head back to the street. "Wait" the butler said. When we turned around I cold see him smiling under his mustache. "I was only kidding boys, come on in"

The house was amazing; it looked like a museum inside. There were pictures and statues everywhere. The pictures were of angels, different than the ones I imagined. The ones on the pictures were much more stunning and they looked so life like.

In the kitchen there were people standing around snacking and talking amongst one another. Everyone was well dressed I must say. I figured that was the reason the butler looked us up and down the way that he did. I had on a black tee shirt as usual, a pair of blue jeans and my black sneakers. Even though we looked out of place with what we had on, no one seemed to care. The people were polite, they greeted us and shook our hands. A man

in a nice black suit approached us. He
introduced himself and told us he was a doctor
and that he wanted to introduce us to some of
his friends. Everyone there was a doctor, a
lawyer, a surgeon, a singer or an actor. It was a
little intimidating but pretty cool at the same
time.

There was a huge clock in the living
room. The hour and minute hands were in the
shape of wings. When it struck 6:36, an alarm
sounded. Everyone headed in the same
direction. Mark and I had no idea what to do
so we just followed the crowd. We entered a
long hallway; the walls on each side were

made of glass. You could see outside bit the

sun rays didn't shine too bright through or

make it too hot. I was checking out all the nice

trees and little animals running around

outside. For some reason I started gazing at my

reflection. I stood there smiling, thinking how

lucky I was to be there. I looked over at Mark's

reflection...there was blood pouring down

from his neck like it had been split open. It

startled me so much I fell to the floor. "What's

wrong dude?" Mark asked as he helped me up.

"Um, nothing I just tripped" I said. Mark knew

something was wrong. He shook his head

"Come on man, we're falling behind"

When we finally caught up with the group, we ended up in a room that was about the size of a basketball court. As I looked around I noticed the room kind of reminded me of a church. There were nice benches to sit on and a podium up front for someone to speak. There were more statues and pictures hanging. There was one particular picture that was mounted on the center of the main wall behind the podium. It was the largest picture in the house. It was a painting of a beautiful angel. It was so amazing; you could see the wisdom and power the picture was portraying.

It looked so realistic; almost felt like it was

staring at me.

Everyone took a seat. Mark and I sat in

the back trying not to draw attention to

ourselves. Once everyone was seated, a man

stepped to the podium, and began to speak...

CHAPTER 19

"Hello everyone, most of you know me already; but for those of you who don't, I would like to introduce myself. My name is Dr. Halstead. Before we get started with today's service, we usually take a little time to give testimony. Some of us share what the spirits have done for us recently. If I am not mistaken, it is my turn to give the first testimony.

Well, this past Wednesday, I had to perform a major, major heart surgery. The patient had been on the donor list for quite some time. My team and I were in the

operating room ready to get started. Before we

began we all held hands as I spoke to the

spirits, asking them to guide my hands

through the procedure. When we let go, I felt

the spirits take control of my hands. They were

moving my arms as if I were their personal

puppet. I opened the patient's chest: I observed

that her heart was at least double in size. While

I was cutting out the old heart, I noticed all the

blood had stopped flowing. There wasn't any

blood to clean up or wipe out of the way. It

made the surgery a lot easier and I was able to

put the new heart in in record speed. We

stitched the patient together and the blood started flowing again as if it never stopped. The patient eventually became stable and as good as new! The word spread about the young woman's surgery and now I have hundreds of patients in line now waiting for me to help them.

(everyone claps)

Thank you, now buy the show of hands, how many of you make at least 6 figures.

(everyone raised their hand, Dr. Halstead smiled)

Now, by the show of hands, how many of you make at least 7 figures.

(Half of the audience raised their hand)

Good, good, now is there anyone that would like to give a testimony for the week?"

A woman raised her hand. She wore big sunglasses and a scarf around her neck. She looked like a movie star. She stood up and walked to the podium…she proceeded to speak…

"Hello everyone, for those of you who don't know me my name is Lauren Lyn. I am a country western singer. I have been in the business for about five years now. In the beginning, my career wasn't going so well. People didn't like my voice and I couldn't get booked for many venues. Earlier in my career,

I used to open up for my best friend Keera. She was a much better singer than I was. We were both 18 then but she could pack a place like no one's business. In her spare time, she would always help me with my music. We would work on things like getting my voice to hit certain notes and she'd help with my guitar playing.

One day we were headed to Dallas, Texas. We decided to drive instead of fly so we could save a little money and have some girl time together. We had a half tank of gas left but she wanted to get off the freeway to fill up anyway. I told her we should keep going but she insisted, claiming she was starving. I sat in

the passenger seat while she pumped the gas.

The nozzle was a little jammed, so she had to

give it a tug to get it out. When it finally gave

way, the gas sprayed everywhere and it got all

over her clothes. she was one of those people

that couldn't get angry at anything if she tried.

She laughed it off and just started to fill up the

tank. As she was filling up a guy came out of

the store; I still remember that mysterious look

he had so vividly. He was holding a soda in

one hand and a lighter in the other. Nothing

too odd at first but I noticed he had a cigarette

hanging rom his lip. I remember everything

feeling like it was going in slow motion. Keera and I were still talking, but I couldn't keep my eyes off of the mysterious man. He looked directly at me as he lit his cigarette; and then turned his sight to Keera. Before I could call her name, he flicked the lit cigarette at her and she caught on fire. Her screams were so agonizing that I fell into shock. I sat there, screaming, not knowing what to do. By the time the fire truck and ambulance arrived, it was too late. Her body was so charred; I couldn't bare to look at her. Something told me to check the armrest before I let the people tow her car away. There was a piece of paper that had the address to this place on it, this church.

I put it in my pocket and let them take the car.

The show had to be canceled so no one got to

see me perform that night. No one ever found

the man, no leads or anything. I started to

come here in hopes that I could follow my best

friend's path. I made it my goal to be just like

her…even better!

I was finally lucky enough to get

booked for a show; seemed like my

opportunity came out of nowhere. The day of

the show I was so excited that I forgot I had

lost my voice the day before. I couldn't cancel

the show; it might have been my only shot. I

remember what I learned here and asked the spirits for help.

When I stepped on stage, I sat in my little chair and held my guitar in my hand. I was so nervous. As my mouth opened, I could see something flying towards me. The closer it got, the clearer it became. It was Keera! My mouth opened more and she flew right in. From the outside it looked like I got hit in the chest by a 300-pound man. All of a sudden, I felt her taking over. I reached for the microphone and with the most beautiful voice…I sang. The crowd went crazy! After that show, I met a record company executive.

He offered me a record deal on the spot. So

here I am ten million dollars later. All thanks to

the spirits"

(Everyone claps)

CHAPTER 20

After hearing Lauren's testimony, I was sold. I pictured myself in my red Ferrari taking Amy on a date to somewhere expensive. I imagined buying her a huge wedding ring and us pulling up to a big mansion. I looked over at Mark but he didn't seem as excited as I was. I could tell by the way he was trying to smile that everything sounded good, but he could tell there was probably some kind of catch. I had so much anxiety built up that I didn't pay attention to the rest of the sermon.

After service, Dr. Halstead approached us. "So what do you guys think?" he asked. I told him the service was nice and how excited I was after I heard the testimony from Lauren. I decided to come right out and ask the question I was itching to ask all day. "So, you all, you all worship the Devil?" Dr. Halstead laughed and put his hands on my shoulder. "Lucifer, yes, our master, he is our lord." "Isn't he evil?" I asked. I could tell he was very prepared for any questions I had.

"Evil, no my friend, he is not evil at all. The story you've heard about, what happened in heaven, it was all a big misunderstanding.

This isn't a battle of good and evil, this is simply a small fight between two sides. One side has their version of the story and the other has theirs. In the end, Jesus will take his people and advocate the world to Lucifer since it is rightfully his anyway. It is against God's nature to destroy Lucifer, so the story you've heard is false." There were so many questions I wanted to ask. "What about hell, isn't God going to send you all to hell?" He slowly nodded. "There are no worries about hell, the spirits can outlive fire. Haven't you seen people walk on fire? Where do you think they get that ability from? You come back next week and think of anything you want the spirits to do for you. When you come back, tell me what you want and it will be given to you."

He handed me a piece of paper. It was an invitation to come back the next Sunday. I was surprised how quiet Mark had been the whole time. As were were walking out the door, Dr. Halstead called for us "Hey boys! Just in case you need something to get back with" he threw us a wad of cash. I flipped my fingers through it and it was 2,500 dollars! Mark's mood seemed to improve once he saw the money. The ride home was quiet at first. Mark stared out the window and I sat there counting my half of the money thinking about what to buy once I got home.

"What's wrong man, you ok?" I wanted to know what was on Mark's mind. "I don't know dude, the Devil? Hell? Is money worth going to hell over? Don't get me wrong, I like the money and I like nice things...but at what cost you know?" The tone of his voice let me know he was very serious. I felt a little different, I mean I had 1,250 dollars in my hand for doing absolutely nothing. No one got hurt, and I didn't have to do anything wrong. I suddenly came up with a clever idea... "How about we just keep the money, and don't get into all that worship and things like that" the

way it came out sounded pretty good in my

opinion, but Mark didn't agree, he didn't say

too much after that. He turned his head and

gazed out the window the rest of the way "I

don't know man" he said softly.

CHAPTER 21

The next day I went to the mall to buy Amy a necklace. I thought a ring would be too much and that a necklace would be much simpler. I found a nice one with diamonds and a heart pendant that I thought would look perfect around her neck. I invited her over that night so I could give it to her.

When she came in she seemed to be a bit nervous. "You ok?" I asked. "Yes I'm fine. I've just been trying to tell you something for the longest now and I never get the opportunity to do it" she said. "Wait me first!" I said grinning.

I pulled out the small box with the necklace

from behind my back and handed it to her.

"What's this?" she asked. "Just open it" I was

smiling from ear to ear in anticipation.

When she opened it, her eyes lit up like

to pretty stars. "This is wonderful Christian,

thank you, where did you get the money for

this?" I told her I had just been saving my

money from the supermarket, she wasn't

aware that I had quit my job yet. She grabbed

me and hugged me tight...she was so warm.

She kicked the door closed and we began to

kiss. She threw the box with the necklace in my

recliner. She stood in front of me and slowly

took her coat off. I leaned forward to kiss her
again and she placed her hand against my
chest. "Wait" she said. she grabbed the bottom
of her shirt and pulled it over her head. I had
never had sex before, so I was a little unsure if
it was my q to take my shirt off too. She
grabbed my shirt and took it off for me. She
jumped in my arms and we started kissing
again. I backed up until we fell on the bed. In
the corner of my eye I could see a book on my
pillow. I grabbed it and placed it on my
nightstand; I was too tied up to wonder why
my Holy Bible ended up on my bed. When I
turned back towards Amy, I saw the figure

standing in the corner of the room. Not

wanting to ruin the mood, a pretended he

wasn't there and continued to kiss Amy. While

we kissed, I heard a deep voice whisper in my

ear…" YOU WERE WARNED" I opened my

eyes and saw that the figure was slowly

walking towards the window. When he flew

out, I thought I was going to have to explain to

Amy, I assumed she heard what was said.

"What is it?" she asked.

Surprisingly, she didn't hear a

thing. We kissed again and for the first time in

my life…I made love. I knew we were too

young, being high school kids and all but it felt so right, so perfect.

Amy had to leave later on that night. As I was giving her a kiss goodbye, Mark came out of his room with a silly grin on his face. He could tell what had just happened. He punched me in the shoulder "Nice" he said. "Anyway, I thought about it and I want to go to the next meeting, or church, or whatever it is they do there. I just want to make what we can and get out. There is no telling what will happen if we stay there forever" I agreed and we decided to return the next Sunday.

CHAPTER 22

Sunday came around again. It was time for our next service. I was up earlier than usual that day thinking about how much we were going to get the next time and the time after that; it made it hard for me to sleep. I got myself dressed a lot earlier than Mark so I decided to catch up on some of my reading. I reached under my chair to grab my book. When I picked it up it was my Holy Bible instead of my Satanic Bible. Why was this book popping up in different places? I was positive that I wasn't the one moving it and I knew there was no one just coming in my room just to move a book.

I figured I might as well check out a chapter or two while I had it in my hand. I opened it to the first page it fell on. It was the book of Ephesians, chapter 4. I quickly turned to chapter 27 "Neither give place to the devil" it read. I remembered the Ouija board at Madam B's house and for some reason I thought about the strange girl I bumped into in the hallway at school. Something was telling me to read more, but when you're engaged in in obsession, there is nothing you can do about it. There was nothing I wanted more than Amy and more money. Mark opened the door and I slid the book back under my chair. I grabbed my jacket and we headed out the door.

Fortunately, we still had enough money to get there and back. It was the same old long ride, but this time, we were both quiet. I started to wonder what the cost would actually be if I kept going down the road I was going. There were still thoughts of the Ouija board in the back of my mind; I knew it was trying to spell Mark when he asked who was going to die next.

When we arrived, the butler let us in with no problems. He didn't say anything, no jokes or anything like the last time. We stood around and ate hors d'oeuvres while we waited for service to start. Every one spoke to us and were polite as usual. Dr. Halstead waved to us from across the room, he had a few men gathered around him. Whatever they were talking about looked important so we didn't interrupt.

When the clock finally struck 6, everyone headed towards the room where service was held. Mark and I sat in the back again hoping no one would call on us to say anything. Dr. Halstead started off service the same way he did the last time. He opened by saying that it was time to give testimony about what the spirits had done for them recently. A man sitting in the middle raised his hand. He was a tall man, black hair wearing a nice looking navy blue suit. He walked to the podium, looked out into the audience, and spoke…

"Good evening everyone, my name is Peter Fenway. I just wanted to take a little time to tell you all what the spirits have done for me this past week. I own a few coffee shops that earn myself a good amount of money. Business has always been good since I have been coming here. As time went by, I had what you might call a gambling problem. Even though I

make over a hundred grand a year, I blow

most of it at the casino. About two weeks ago, I

decided to ask the spirits for help. They had

already been helping me with my coffee shops

but I wanted more. I wanted to win big at the

casino. I needed the high from winning. So I

asked for help with Blackjack, its my favorite

table game. Last Wednesday, I took about ten

grand with me and went to the casino. Before I

went in, I talked to the spirits reminding them

what I had asked for *(he laughs)* When I got to the

table, I put down one hundred dollars on my

first bet. The dealer deals me a fifteen and he

has a seven. Naturally I take a hit, I bust. Now I'm really upset because I thought the spirits ignored my request but something told me to put more money down the next hand. I put down two grand on the next hand and I won ten straight black jacks! At the end of the night I walked out of there with one hundred grand! I made a year's worth of salary in that one night. I am proof of what the spirits can do for you!" *(Everyone claps)*

Whatever doubts Mark and I had were clearly forgotten about at that moment. We turned towards each other "One hundred grand" we said at the same time. I tried to pay attention to the rest of the service. The huge picture behind the podium kept giving me the creeps. It seemed like it was looking at me. Whoever painted it was an excellent artist; the painting looked almost too real. Dr. Halstead walked back to the podium and began the sermon…it was a sermon I would never forget.

"Today we are going to discuss a few important points. The master has guided me into discussion for today because he wanted everyone to be clear of our mission. If we don't follow it to the letter we will fail. Does anyone know about the Great Council that was held back in the 1700's? Well, the master is a wise

individual. He has studied the Holy Bible more
than anyone in human history. The Great
Council held back then regarded a plan. The
master and his angels devised a way whereby
people would basically disqualify themselves
from being members of Christ's kingdom.
There were three policies discussed, and I will
go over them with you. Policy number one:
Deceive the people about the angels and
Lucifer's existence. If you don't believe in the
existence of Lucifer, why would you have a
reason to believe in the Creator? If you can
discredit one thing in the Bible, you can
discredit the entire book. Now, have we been

successful in that area? Survey says 75% of people don't believe in a tangible devil; that is astounding numbers my friends. Policy number 2: Take control over the minds of people through hypnotism. The plan was to take it out of the realm of the occult and introduce it as a science for the benefit of mankind. The term mesmerism was brought about. It basically stated that people had some kind of magnetism, which allowed them to put a "trans" on others. It was and is widely accepted by the public. *(He laughs)* People really believe anything don't they? People actually believe the Earth is billions and billions of years old. If you do the math, from the time of

creation, the Earth is only six thousand years

old. Can you believe that?

Policy number 3: Policy number 3 says

we must destroy the Bible…without burning it.

Now, how do we accomplish that? The master

chose Charles Darwin. He personally taught

him how to set up the principles of the Theory

of Evolution. If a person believes in evolution,

it destroys the creation week in the Holy Bible,

the fall of man, and the plan of redemption.

Anyone who teaches the Theory of Evolution is

considered to be a master of our great religious

system. He is of great value; he will receive

unction from Lucifer himself and will receive great power with the ability to convert, convince, and to induce spiritual blindness. He will also be assigned angels to follow him the rest of his life, which is considered the greatest gift from the master.

I also wanted to go over, who all her is familiar with Lucis Trust located in the United Nations? Well, Lucis Trust was known before as Lucifer Trust. It was founded by Alice A. Bailey. She is considered one of our greatest leaders in our religion. In one of her 25 esoteric books, she came up with the Ten Strategies to Get Occult Principles to be accepted by the world. This was a plan carefully thought out and guided by the master. In my opinion, it is genius.

Number one: Push God out of schools, if people grow up without a reference to God, they will consider God irrelevant.

Number two: Break traditional Christian family concepts. Break communication between parents and children so that parents can't pass on spiritual values to their children. You accomplish this by pushing excessive child rights.

Number three: Remove restrictions on sex. Sex is the biggest joy and Christianity robs people of this. People must be free to enjoy it without restrictions. It is not just for the married, it is for everybody!

Number Four: Sex is the greatest expression of a mans enjoyment of life. Man must be free to express sex in all of its forms; homosexuality, orgies, even beastiality are desirable as long as no one is harmed or abused.

Number Five: People must be free to abort unwanted children.

Number Six: Every person develops soul bonds. Therefore, when a soul bond wears out, a person must be free to divorce. When one starts to grow one must be free to get together with that person even if they are married.

Number Seven: Defuse religion radicalism.

Christianity says Jesus is the only way; defuse

this by a) silencing Christianity and b)

promoting other faiths, which brought about

the creation of interfaith harmony.

Number Eight: Use the media to influence

mass opinion. Create mass opinion that is

receptive to these values by using TV, Film, the

press and so forth. Note, what western

believers call normal, in the African church

would be considered pornography.

Number Nine: Debase art in all of its forms.

Corrupt music, paintings, poetry to every

expression of the heart and make it obscure, immoral and occultic. Debase the arts in every way possible…and Number Ten: Get the church to endorse all nine strategies. Get the church to accept these principles and say that they are ok. Then legal ground is given for these values to get a foothold.

Good stuff huh? Our plan is being followed to a T. There is no doubt in my mind that we will be victorious. I don't want to keep you all day, but I want to go over one more topic.

I want to talk about the grand plan before the end of the great controversy. People are going to eat this up. Angels will declare themselves to be inhabitants of far distant planets. A threat will be made that people will be destroyed if they don't follow the instructions given to them. Then angels will give guidance in avoiding the destruction of the planet and cause it to enter a higher state of existence. A glorious new age of peace and prosperity will come to last one thousand years if instructions are carried out correctly. There will be no wars, no famine, no social unrest, just love. As the times get harder and harder the angels will impress the importance of Sunday sacredness. Laws will be passed to honor Sunday. The police will explain to the masses that the law is necessary to assure the wellbeing of all people.

Now I know that was a lot for one day, but does anyone have any questions?" A man in the middle of the audience raised his hand... "Is it true the spirits helped the founder of Coca Cola?" he asked. "Yes it is one hundred percent true. You see Coca Cola had a deal with the master. The master told him, I will make you the number one business, the most powerful on Earth, but every month you must offer me three souls in sacrifice. Those souls ended up being sacrificed and bottled. This came out with a guy in Germany many years ago. He found fingers and the remains of flesh inside bottles of coke. It was a price he was willing to pay to be powerful and wealthy."

Another man in the audience raised his hand..." What about Adventists? How do they play a role in our plan when they observe the Sabbath?" "Oh yea, the Adventists. Most Adventists cannot be brought under our great deception. However, it really doesn't matter since there are only a few of them. The fact that they observe the day of the creator makes it very difficult for the spirits to deceive them. They are not ordinary people; they have spiritual insight. But they are nothing to worry about. Now, are there any more questions?" Dr. Halstead asked. No hands were raised.

"Good good, I think we covered a lot today. I think we all know now that we have a lot of work to do, for the time is short at hand…. thank you" he said as he stepped down from the podium.

CHAPTER 23

When the sermon was over, I sat there in disgust. I wanted more money with all of my soul, but hearing the plans of those people disturbed me to the core. The sad thing is I knew I'd probably continue coming. Everything in my heart said I should leave that place and never look back. I looked over at Mark and he was just staring at the huge picture on the main wall. I saw a tear falling down his cheek, I knew he was scared. He looked back at me and shook his head "I can't

do it bro; this can't be right" I shook my head
as if I agreed with him.

We got up to leave and before we
reached the front door, Dr. Halstead stopped
us. "Hey boys, I know what was a lot to digest
today. Might have been a little overwhelming.
But the master tells me you boys are more than
ready to join our army and help us fight for or
cause. I am inclined to tell you that after today,
how can I put this...there is no way out. You
are part of our family now. No worries boys,
the spirits will make it worth your while" As
he was finishing up his motivational speech, I
could feel him slipping something in my

pocket. I knew it was money. He knew the kind of money he was giving us would blind us…and he was right.

Dr. Halstead sent us home in a limo instead of us taking a cab. During the ride, I could see Mark trying to hold himself back from crying. "You ok?" I asked. He took a second to respond "Did you hear any of that in there? Do you see what they are doing to us, doing to everyone? I like money Christian, but I can't go to hell over it" I didn't know how to respond, I knew I was going back. "So there's no way you're going back there, not even to see what the spirits can do for you?" I asked

him. "No way" he said, he meant it.

When he said that, I got a chill up my

spine. A small breeze entered into the back of

the limo. I looked around and noticed none of

the windows were down. I got the feeling that

something was about to happen to Mark. I saw

the seat next to him indent like someone had

just sat down. I closed my eyes balled up my

fists and YELLED! "NO!" My eyes were still

closed but I didn't hear anything. I slowly

opened them and Mark was staring at me like I

was crazy. "Dude, you need some serious

medication. I forgot I had to go to my

grandmothers today, I wonder if the driver will drop me off there" He knocked on the glass that separated us from the driver and asked him if it was ok if he could be dropped off at a different address. The driver agreed and gave him a thumbs up. I was a little embarrassed but I was relieved that nothing happened to him. He was my only friend and I would hate for anything to happen to him.

When we reached our first destination, I noticed it was a little darker outside than usual. Mark gave me a high five and then got out of the car. The limo driver waited until he made it in the house. I figured he wanted to make sure that he didn't have to come back. I forgot to give Mark half of the money I had in my pocket. "Mark!" I called out to him. He turned around and saw the money I was holding in my hand. He headed back towards the car but stopped in the middle of the street. "Just toss it to me, I don't feel like walking all the way over there." I laughed and took his half, reached my arm out the window and tossed him the wad of money. Before his fingertips could get a hold of it, an SUV slammed into Mark. It came by so fast; it looked like Mark had exploded on contact. There was blood everywhere and money floating in the air. The truck didn't even turn around to see what happened.

"NOOOOOOOOOOOOOOOOO" I screamed. I jumped out of the limo and fell to the ground next to what was left of him. I cried until I could barely breathe, knowing there was nothing I could do. I looked up and saw the figure standing on top of Mark's grandmothers house. He knew I was looking at him and I felt him looking right back. At that moment I hated him with every cell in my body. Mark was the only friend I ever had and he took that away from me. I'm sure it was the wrong decision at the time, but I knew I was going to make all the money I could from the spirits and then I was going to leave that God forsaken place.

I wasn't scared of being harmed. I figured if he was going to hurt me he would've already done it. I never knew why he followed me in the first place but from then on I didn't care anymore. My obsession with the Devil became even stronger. The limo driver blew his horn and I got back in the vehicle. I ignored the fact that he was being heartless and hopped in. I didn't want to be bothered with the police anyway.

When I got back home, I walked straight in my room. There was blood all over my pants and non one even noticed. I sat in my chair and

started thinking. There was something that had

to be done, I just couldn't figure out what it

was.

CHAPTER 24

It was finally time for prom, the time of year all seniors in high school dream about. All the tuxedos and cars and the excitement was all about one particular day. I admit, I was just as excited as everyone else. And why not? I had the captain of the cheerleading squad as my date. By this time, I had enough money to do whatever I wanted. I had an expensive suit, a Rolls Royce for the weekend, it felt like I had it all.

It had been a few weeks since Mark was murdered. He had been reported missing but no detectives or anyone asked me anything. I was untouchable.

I had been going back to the church listening to Dr. Halstead speak. Within that time, I had asked the spirits for more money. I asked only once, but when I asked I asked for Fifty thousand dollars. Wasn't sure if I was supposed to go to a casino or play the lottery, I had no clue. When I got home from service, that day, I went to my room to ponder on how to get the money. Surprisingly, when I opened the door, there were hundred dollar bills piled up in the middle of my bed. On top of the pile was a small note "FOR YOU" it read. I threw the note away and gathered all my money together. All I wanted was to take. I left right back out and took myself shopping.

Prom began at Seven. I got myself dressed around Four thirty in the afternoon while Amy got dressed at home. I knew I would be dressed a lot earlier than her so I decided to catch a little nap since I was in for a long night. I reclined back in my chair and closed my eyes. I had some crazy dreams before, but the one I had that day was a dream I would never forget.

My eyes opened, I knew I was still in a dream. I sat on a bench in what looked like to be Aleister's woods. I stood up to leave but there was a voice "Sit down" it said. When I looked back it was an angel. He was dressed in white and he had a beautiful glow around him. He had wings like the figure but I knew it wasn't him. I sat down next to him. There was a book in his hand. He opened it and put half of it on my lap to make sure I could see. "Here is wisdom" he said. When I looked in the book I saw a Catholic priest. He was dressed in the usual white garments. "I don't understand" I said to the angel. "Keep looking" he responded. I looked again and saw the priest changing clothes. He put on a black robe with the words "The Brotherhood" written on the back. He dipped his hand in some kind of tray and made an upside down cross on a woman's forehead. Suddenly the words flashed, Defeat, Rebellion, Christ, and then I saw some kind of figure that looked like a man hanging from a cross. I had no idea what I was looking at but I needed to see more. The angel turned the page, next page was blank for a second and then words started typing themselves on the page. "Count the number of the beast" it read. Then one at a time a 6 appeared on the page until it was three of them. Two of them disappeared and the remaining 6 turned into a pair of dice. I saw the dice had six sides and had the

numbers one through six. The dice turned into

dominoes, I saw the dominoes went up to the

number six. The angel turned the page again.

The next page was an empty chess board. The

board took up both pages. In the top left corner

of the left page was the word Christians, on the

opposite side it said Satan's Army. "There is a

war" the angel said "They represent members

of the satanic sects; they are sent out to all the

congregations." The rook appeared "They

represent the Catholic Church, who protects

the satanic sects" the bishop appeared "The

Pope" The knights appeared "They will arise

two demons, and they will fight against Christ during his second coming" the queen appeared "The queen, she represents the Satanic sects, you see how she is protected" Finally the king appeared "The king, he is Lucifer, the Devil" I stared at the king and it started to change shape. It formed into the figure I've known all my life. I balled up my fist and tried to strike the book. Before my fist hit the book, my cell phone ran and I woke up.

Amy was calling the time then was 6 pm. I didn't realize I had slept for so long. She told me that she had one stop to make and that she would call me when she was on her way home so I could meet her there. It seemed a little late to have made one stop. I knew her family wanted to take pics of us before we left.

"Oh I have a surprise for you too" she said. "Oh yea, are you going to tell me or are you going to keep it a secret like the thing you were supposed to tell me a million years ago" I said smiling. Her voice suddenly lost its excitement "You're right, I'm sorry about that, I just never found the right time to say, I promise I will tell you when you pick me up" she said. I said ok and we hung up.

It was 7pm and Amy still hadn't called me back. I decided to drive over to her house. I thought she might have still been getting

dressed, she was always slow when it came to

those things. On the way there I noticed the

sky was darker than normal. It reminded me of

the day Mark died. Hopefully the darkness just

meant there was a little rain coming. Even

though it was the day of prom, rain would've

been a lot better than the alternative.

I pulled up to Amy's house and saw her

mom on the porch crying and talking to a

police officer. I waited in the car until he left. I

didn't want to answer any questions about

Mark. When he left, I approached Amy's mom,

she was still standing there with her face

buried in her hands. "What's wrong Mrs.

Hunter?" I asked. She opened her arms for me

to hug her. Hugging her reminded me of the

hug Amy gave me when Brad passed away.

"Christian" she said, she could barley

get her words out "Its Amy, she got into a car

accident" I quickly pushed her away "What?" I

yelled. "She's at the hospital now, I'm waiting

for her dad so we can ride up there together"

she said.

I ran to my car and headed to the

hospital. I must have been doing ninety miles

an hour the whole way there. I pulled up to the

front of the hospital and ran in. I was in such a rush that I left the car running.

When I reached the receptionist I asked what room Amy was in. "And you are" she asked. "I'm her brother, I heard she got in a car accident" I quickly responded. She pointed down the hallway "She's in room 106". I ran down the hallway as she was trying to hand me the sign in sheet. When I got to her room I saw that she was bloody and bruised. She had oxygen tubes stuck in her nose. I grabbed her by the hand hoping she would wake up. "Amy" I called her name but she didn't respond. "Amy please" I tried again, her eyes opened. She smiled as best as she could

"Christian, I'm sorry baby, I should've been

paying more attention" She started to cry as I

rubbed her hand and told her not to worry

about anything and that everything was going

to be ok. "Christian, I have to tell you

something, its important" A small breeze

passed through the room. I looked around

expecting to see the figure but he was no

where to be found. "Just get some rest, you can

tell me when you get better" I said while I kept

rubbing her hand. "NO, I have to tell you now!

Please. Remember the house fire you were in

when you were a kid?" "Yea, what does that

have to do with anything?" I asked. "Well, I looked up the article the night you told me, the story doesn't match up Christian." "What do you mean?" I asked. "Christian, who was in the house that night?" "Me, my mom, and my dad". "Christian, it said it was just you and your mom, they didn't mention anything about your dad". "Amy, what are you talking about?" I asked confused. "There is no record of your dad, anywhere"

I tried to remember everything I could about my father and I couldn't come up with anything. Who he was…who was the man that walked out of my house that night? Amy began to cough and it looked like she was in a lot of pain. I kneeled down loser to her, trying to comfort her. I saw the figure standing in the corner of the room, I knew why he was there. I tried to keep myself from crying and looked back at Amy. I stroked her hair as she was trying to speak again.

"Its one more thing I had to tell you" she coughed and the heart monitor started to beep slower. "Yes, what is it" I asked softly. "I'm pregnant" she said as the heart monitor flat lined.

I let go of her hand and turned around expecting to see the Devil still standing in the corner, but he had already vanished. I wiped my tears and grabbed a piece of paper that was sticking out of Amy's purse. I opened it and it was the old article she was talking about. The house was only ten minutes away from where I was. I knew what I had to do. I left the hospital the same time her parents arrived. They ran right past me; they must've heard the news. Surprisingly, my car was still in the font running so I got in and headed towards the house. I had a million emotions running through me. I had no idea what to expect when I got there. I didn't know if it was going to be a new house there or just a pile of ash.

The house was still standing when I got there. Most of it was blackened by the fire. I couldn't help but to wonder why it was still standing after all that time. I stood at the front door and said some words to myself that I should have said months ago "God help me". Its hard to describe what I felt after I said it but I literally felt a huge amount of pressure lifted from my shoulders. I walked in the house unafraid, not knowing what I was looking for, or what I would find.

I saw the upstairs had fallen downstairs, just like I remembered. I kicked around a few two by fours and trash that was on the floor. I flipped over things, kicked some things out of

the way, looking for anything.

I was standing next to the kitchen and

noticed an envelope sticking out of a pile of

ash. It was a little strange because it looked

brand new. It wasn't burned or anything when

I picked it up. I opened it…it was addressed to

me.

CHAPTER 25

"Dear son,

If you ever find this letter, I will probably probably be long gone from this world. There are some things I must share with you that you need to know and may disturb you.

First of all, you need to know I am your mother and I love you very much. I love you more than anything in this world.

When I was a little girl, I grew up very poor. I never had nice things like new clothes, new shoes or anything like the other kids had.

Every day was a struggle for your

grandmother and I. Each day I watched her go

to work just to make enough money for us to

eat once a day. Every night I would go to bed

starving because all I had that day was a slice

of bread and a cup of water. There were plenty

of times we didn't have electricity and we had

to make a small fire in the living room to keep

warm.

When I turned seventeen, I started to

see a man everywhere I went. I would see him

when I left school, when I went to the store,

even when I walked out of church at times. He

reminded me of a lion, studying his prey until it was the right time to move. In the beginning, he never spoke. Every time I looked at him, it felt like his eyes were hypnotizing me. It was weird, but secretly, I always enjoyed it. The attraction for him grew by the day. Every day I hoped I would see him again and maybe he would have the courage to speak to me.

The day I turned eighteen, I finally got my wish. I was leaving the local malt shop with some friends one night. I heard someone call my name as I was crossing the street. He was standing by a light pole waiting for me. I didn't know how he knew my name but I was to flattered to care. He asked if I minded if he walked me home. I told my friends they could leave and that I would catch up with them the next day.

We walked, we talked, and he wanted to know everything about me. Every time I would ask him something about himself, he would just ask me another question about me. I loved to talk so I didn't mind. He was more handsome up close than I ever imagined. He almost seemed to have a glow about himself. His eyes were full of wisdom and he spoke with a lot of intelligence. When we finally got to my door, he stole my heard with two words

"You're perfect" I remember it like it was yesterday.

Every day after that he walked me everywhere I went. He would already be waiting outside my door when I left in the morning. He loved the morning sun; he once told me the sun was like his father and how beautiful it felt on his back. He would always joke around saying people should worship the sun. I was intrigued by the poetic way he would speak at times.

One day he told me he could take me away from the life I was living. There would be no or pain, no more struggling, no more hunger, no more thirst. I was so desperate and in love I was willing to do anything he wanted me to do. He only asked for one thing in return. He said he wanted the honor of being the father of my first child and that he wanted me to give him the perfect baby boy. I would soon learn what he meant when he said "give me". Nevertheless, I agreed so he asked me to go to church with him one Sunday. He told me how he loved Sunday and that it was his favorite day of the week. To my surprise, we went to a Catholic church. I met with the priest, he was an old man dressed in a black tunic. They invited me to "Ash Wednesday" where my love told me we would officially

start our beginning together.

When that day came, there was a

ceremony. The priest was speaking in Latin

and he rubbed black ash on my forehead.

When the ceremony was over, I had to use the

restroom. As I washed my hands I noticed the

cross on my forehead upside down.

My love insisted that we get married the

next day. I was nervous, but there wasn't

anything I wouldn't do for him. We got

married the next day and made passionate love

that night. It was the most memorable

experience I ever encountered.

During the next eight months, I experienced things I never thought were possible. I lived in a house so huge It could fill up a football field. I had all the cars, clothes, jewelry and money anyone could imagine. I must say, during those months I can look back and say I was not proud of myself. I forgot where I came from; all the values I learned as a young woman were gone. I began to think I was better than everyone else and people didn't even deserve to walk on the same ground as I did. It was a proud and lonely world for me. I lost all the friends I had, even lost contact with my mother. All I had was the company of your father. You were born

October 31st. You and your father shared

birthdays, I thought that was so weird how

that turned out.

I was so drugged up at the hospital that

I had your father fill out the birth certificate.

Your name was supposed to be Christian

Lawrence Smith. When your birth certificate

arrived in the mail, I noticed your middle

name was not what I told your father to record.

Your certificate read that your name was

Christian Lucifer Smith. I hadn't read the Bible

but I had been to church enough to know who

the Devil was. When I confronted your father

about your name, he told me in a very calm manner, it was time that I gave you to him. He told me that he was taking you and would be leaving forever. There was no way I was going to let that happen. His arrogant response was only "a deal is a deal" I asked him what deal?

You see my son, all the money, the cars, the house, it all came with a price...and that price was my soul...and you. Your father is a deceiver and a liar. If you ever see him again, please stay away from him! Pray and ask God to protect you and show you the truth. By now, you should know your father's name. His name Christian...is Lucifer.

Even though he is your father in the flesh, he is not your true father. Your one and only true father is the father in heaven. ALWAYS REMEMBER THAT. You see in the end I realized and learned a few things. Lucifer loved Sunday so much because he himself placed and unction, authority and power on Sunday. He deliberately chose the first day of the week as his day because the creator chose the last day of the week to sanctify. He despises the father in heaven and will go to the ends of the Earth to take us away from him. Do not worship on Sunday Christian, no matter who you claim to worship on that day you are paying homage to the Devil. He loved the sun so much because he convinced people ages to ago to worship the sun instead of the creator. It was a small victory for him. He also bore the name "the sun of the morning" when he lived in heaven. Do not consult with the queen of heaven or the signs of the zodiac. My son those are occult practices, they are traps, tricks of the Devil. Everyone who involves themselves with these things lives their lives daily with insecurities.

Last but not least my son, the Devil does not work alone. He has brothers, demons rather. Now beware of them…there are three kinds. You have friendly ones; those are the ones that aren't upset about what happened in heaven. You have warriors, they like to bring destruction to our planet. Lastly you have oppressors, they hate the father in heaven and with every cell in their body and live to terrorize the human race. Now by all means do not be fooled by the friendly spirits. They pride themselves in impersonating the dead. Do not be deceived in believing you will be able to contact me after I am gone. Read the Bible my son, no human soul is immortal. Only the chosen ones who give their lives to Christ will live again and live forever!

The human race has been taught to believe in necromancy. That is the belief that we all have an immortal soul and that we enter a higher state of being after we die that was better than life on Earth. You do not have to call on any demons for help in this area, all you have to do is believe in life after death and you've already fallen for what the Devil likes to call, Christian idolatry. Son it breaks another commandment as the Sunday worship does. It is all in the plan to disqualify us from entering into heaven.

I love you son and I urge you to seek the truth, do not let the Devil deceive you as he has done to me. I don't know what he is going to do to me, but I'm sure my time is short. I broke the deal and refused to give you up. I would break that deal again and again and a million times over. Do not forget me son, you are special, you always were and you always will be.

Love,

Your mother"

CHAPTER 26

After reading my mothers letter, I knew then what had to be done. I was tired of the lies, tired of the killing…it was time to stood up to my father face to face. I didn't know where to find him but without a doubt…it was time.

I left the burned house with no destination in mind. A thunderstorm began to fall. There was lightning everywhere. I had one thing and one thing only on my mind. I walked and I walked until I ended up at the high school. I walked towards the back where the

football field was. I could feel him; I knew he
was close. I stood in the middle of the field as
the rain poured down heavily. The thunder
was so loud the sound of it brought pain to my
ears. Lightning struck near by, but I didn't
care. I yelled as loud as I could "WHERE ARE
YOU!"

The loudest crack of thunder rang
across the sky. I looked up and saw a ball of
light headed towards me. As it got closer it
became larger and larger. It was so bright it
became unbearable to look at. As it slowly died
down it formed into the figure I was
desperately waiting to see. This time he wasn't

the black figure I was used to seeing. I saw

every detail about him. His wings were white

and enormous; he had a breastplate encrusted

with different stones. His body was built like

one of the statues you see in Rome. His

face...his face looked almost like mine. He had

black hair and his eyes were as red as fire. We

must've stared at each other for at least five

minutes. I knew it would be useless to just

attack him. I took a deep breath, and finally got

the courage to speak

"So you're really the Devil huh"

"My name is Lucifer, but you my son, can call

me dad"

"Why have you been following me? Why did you kill all those people?"

"I've protected you your whole life. Anyone that caused you harm, anyone that wanted to take you from me I destroyed! Like any father would do for his son.

"But why my mother? Why her? Why us?!"

"I needed a son. I need you to help me lead my army in the battle that is to come. My brothers are soldiers but they are not leaders, as you are my son. Together we will triumph!"

"Battle? What battle?

"I'm sure you've heard of our battle, with them" He looked up to the sky.

"With God?" I asked

"Of course, but your book is inaccurate,

because we will be victorious!" Every word he

spoke was with much confidence.

"Why should I believe anything you tell me?"

"Is this an interview?" he said laughing.

"I read the Bible. I read the letter from my

mother, they all say you are a liar...a deceiver!

You deceived the angels in Heaven, and you

deceived my mother!"

"Deceived! What do you know about deceit?!

HE IS THE DECEIVER!!" He pointed up as

thunder roared across the night sky.

"What did you do?" I asked. He looked at me with much anger in his eyes. His chest rose with every breath he took…" I will show you" he responded. He looked up at the sky; his wings spread as far as they could stretch. The rain around me stopped. It was still coming down but it was like I had an invisible shelter over me. I started feeling drowsy, my legs were getting weak…I fell to my knees. "What are you doing to me?" I asked with the last bit of energy I had left. He whispered "Be calm, open your eyes and see" I fell face first into the grass and fell into a deep, deep sleep.

CHAPTER 27

When my eyes opened, there were white clouds everywhere. I saw walkways made of gold and everything was extremely bright. I slowly started to walk down one of the golden pathways. There were angels dressed in white flying around but none of them seemed to notice me. They were all headed in one direction so I followed them. Voices began to ring throughout the skies. The more I walked, the louder they got. They were a little distance ahead of me but I could still see the direction they were headed. It was no way to tell how long I had walked or what distance I had covered but I eventually entered an area that embodied the most beautiful site my eyes could've ever imagined. I saw the throne of God! I knew what it was because I remembered reading about it. There was one angel covering the throne with its wings. I moved in a little closer to see more detail, it was Lucifer! His wings covered the entire seat of God. They covered so much so that no one was able to see who sat in the throne. There was an incredible rainbow that arched over the large seat. There were twenty-four seats that surrounded the area and in each seat sat an old man dressed in white. They all were wearing gold crowns on their heads. Thunder, lightning, and voices chanting covered the skies. I noticed seven lamps sitting in front of the throne. They were all lit and none of the fires were attached to a wick, it was as if the fires were floating within them. A sea of glass stretched as far as my eyes could see. There were huge beasts surrounding the throne…but not just any ordinary animals. They all had wings; the first beast looked like a lion, the second looked like a calf, the third had the face of a man and the fourth had the face of an eagle. Everything I was witnessing was becoming a little overwhelming.

I watched Lucifer standing there doing his duty as an angel. He looked so pleased to be doing his task. Out of nowhere, I heard the voice of God...the depth of his voice was so deep I could feel my body vibrating. "Lucifer, gather your brothers, for it is time for worship." "Yes Lord" he responded. When he flew away the light that he was covering on throne traveled with him. It was like watching the sun fly. He flew to each corner of Heaven, gathering the other angels. They all obeyed his commands. God was like the General, and

Lucifer was the colonel. As Lucifer was

gathering the rest of the angels I heard God

speak to himself "It is time, the test must be

done" When Lucifer returned to the throne,

God spoke again "Lucifer, thou are the

anointed cherub that covereth. I have set thee

so. Thou rest upon the Holy mountain of God,

thou hast walked up and down in the midst of

the stones of fire. I have made thou perfect in

every way since the day of your creation. I

have covered you with every precious stone"

"Yes Lord, I thank thee" Lucifer responds.

"The time has come; it is time to anoint once

again an angel of Heaven. He will rule all of

Heaven by my side. To what I ask, shall I grant

him? I will let thou think to thyself. Bring back

your answer when thou hast finished."

"Yes Lord" he flew away to a place where he

could be alone and think to himself. He paced

back and forth, wondering what he should say.

Suddenly, he had an idea. "The Lord must be

referring to me. I am the closest thing to the

creator. The angelic host already obey my

every command. He is going to make me a

king! And a king, deserves to be worshipped!"

He flew back to the throne ready to give God

his answer.

"Lucifer, does thou have an answer" God asked.

"Yes Lord. I believe your anointed one should receive worship, as you do"

"WORSHIP? I AM GOD!" God says as thunder roared. Lucifer few back to his secluded place wondering what he has just done. He was afraid to go back. He rested there until he heard his name called again. "Yes Lord"

"I have considered your suggestion. The anointed one shall receive worship. Gather your brothers and I shall announce it to all of the Heavens.

"YES MY LORD!"

"I will need another cherub to cover the throne while you are away. Bring Michael to take your place."

Lucifer was a little confused by the command. Michael was just an ordinary angel. He was a smaller and humbler looking angel in comparison to the others. As God asked, he fetched Michael and gave him the command to watch the throne. He obeyed and flew to his new place of duty. Without any question, he kneeled; he spread his wings and covered the throne.

In the meantime, Lucifer gathered all the angels of Heaven. He was so excited about the announcement that was coming. He wanted it to be a surprise so he didn't speak of it to anyone.

It took about an hour for all the angels to gather in one place for the ceremony. There were thousands upon thousands of angels gathered, too many to count. They all stood there, waiting on God to speak.

When Lucifer returned to the throne, he and Michael stood in front of the seat equal distance apart. Michael stood to the right and Lucifer to the left. They faced each other and at that moment it looked exactly like the replica the Lord told Moses to build in a story I read.

A trumpet blew and there was silence in Heaven for at least thirty minutes. The angels stood at attention; they had incredible discipline. Finally, God spoke...

"My children I have gathered you all here to honor and glorify our new anointed one. He shall receive worship as I. He will rule the Heavens side by side with me. He will be one with me...A GOD." Lucifer patently waited for the moment he had been yearning for.

"My children, I hereby proclaim..." Lucifer begins to take a step forward

"MICHAEL! HE SHALL BE THE ANOINTED ONE. You shall worship him as you worship me! He will rule the Heavens side by side with me."

I saw the instant rage that fell upon Lucifer. "Michael?" he said to himself. The entire angelic host bowed and worshipped the newly anointed one...except for Lucifer. God spoke to him "Lucifer, bow to your Lord, as I have asked of you" he looked towards Michael with disgust...and then he bowed. He stared at the ground, his eyes were filled with tears as he gritted his teeth. I could see how deep his pain was.

Michael received worship form the angels as the Lord had asked. They were all chanting "HOLY HOLY HOLY LORD GOD ALMIGHTY, WHICH WAS, AND IS, AND IS TO COME. THOU ART WORTHY O LORD TO RECEIVE GLORY AND HONOR AND POWER, FOR THOU HAST CREATED ALL THINGS, AND FOR THEY PLEASURE THEY ARE AND WERE CREATED"

Michael and Lucifer returned to their positions at before the seat when the worship service was over. Lucifer's anger soon turned into an empty, soul-less look. I thought he was going to ask God why Michael was chosen over him, instead, he said nothing.

A short while later, Lucifer asked to be excused from his position. I thought he wanted to fly to his place of thinking but instead he flew all throughout Heaven, talking to other angels. He accused God of unfair treatment to him and the entire angelic host. He told them they were as slaves and had no free will; that they were like animals waiting to be told what to do. He charged Michael for going behind everyone's back making everyone look bad o the Lord so that he could be the anointed one. Back at the throne, Michael head God let out a sigh..." What's wrong my Lord" he asked.

Choice | James Green

"I need you to bring Lucifer, so that I may speak to him" "Yes Lord" Michael said.

Michael flew through Heaven in search for Lucifer. When he found him, he was in the center of a few thousand angels speaking. Michael couldn't hear what was being said but he didn't concern himself with it. He passed the message to Lucifer and returned to the throne.

When Lucifer returned, half of the angelic host followed behind him. He didn't kneel…he stood, as if he were the new father of his brothers.

"Lucifer" God said

"Yes…" Lucifer responded.

"Thou hast committed a sin; thou art the accuser of the brethren, why hast thou done so? Michael, please stand before thy brothers of Heaven." Michael took a few steps forward and stood before the angels. God spoke again, "BEHOLD! MICHAEL, THE ARCHANGEL, AND SON OF GOD. He is me and I am him. To have served him, you have served me. He was not created as I have created you. He is the living test, the proof of love and loyalty. I know of who has joined your brother Lucifer in false accusing my son. This is your time to repent, and worship…and I shall forgive."

The angels looked at each other, surprised and slightly afraid. None of them had ever sinned before and they knew the price of doing so. I want able to read Lucifer's feelings. I wasn't sure if he regretted what he had done and his pride was taking over, or he just didn't care. Why didn't he just obey? He was the closest thing to God. Anything he wanted would have been given to him if he had just been loyal. It was pride, that was the beginning of his downfall.

God commanded Lucifer to bow. He told him that he would be forgiven. He stood there, chest poking out proudly. He looked behind him and saw a third of the angels still by his side. With the amount of loyal followers he had there was no turning back "I SHALL NOT BOW! I WILL EXALT MY THRONE ABOVE THE STARS OF YOU! I WILL SIT UPON THE MOUNT OF THE CONGREGATION, IN THE SIDES OF THE NORTH. I WILL ASCEND ABOVE THE HEIGHTS OF THE CLOUDS…I WILL BE THE LIKE THE MOST HIGH!"

Everything began to shake. Fire began to surround the throne. The angels hid behind their wings as the fire became larger, brighter and hotter. The sound of thunder roared and there was a flash.

When the brightness died down, everyone turned to look. Everyone expected to see Lucifer destroyed. He was still standing, covered by the wing of Michael…who was willing to give his life to save him. Lucifer patted himself, seemingly surprised to still be alive. He let out a loud, evil laugh. His followers joined him in his joy. "Thou art weak. Thou dost not deserve to sit upon the throne!"

Somehow could see what God was thinking. If he destroyed Lucifer, the rest of the angelic host would serve out of fear instead of love. God didn't wan tot see that happen. He called to Michael…" Michael, Lucifer, the accuser is now called Satan, the Devil, he shall not dwell in the Heavens ever again…ATTACK!"

And there was war in Heaven. Michael and his angels fought against Lucifer and his angels. Lucifer and one third of the angles that followed him did not prevail; they were cast out of Heaven and fell to the Earth. And as quick as they were cast out, I fell to Earth with them…and then I woke up.

I was still a little drowsy but at that moment, things were as clear as they had ever been.

CHAPTER 28

"Now do you see my son. I was treated as a peasant, and I shall have my revenge. My soldiers are trained and with you by my side, we will not lose again" Lucifer said.

"Why me? I am not an angel, what could I possibly have to offer you?" I asked.

"You are they key my son; the son of God shall face the son of the Dragon. You are prophecy fulfilled. You shall serve, as the Anti-Christ!

"Anti-Christ?" I responded.

"Do not worry, much is rewarded to whom serves me. I am fair, I am here! I give to who worship me whatever he desires! I don't lead from afar and treat others unfairly. I will give you your Amy back. I will give you all the riches your mind can imagine. All these things I will give thee…if thou wilt fall down and worship me!"

That moment, my life seemed to flash before my eyes. I thought about my mother and her words, Amy…and what he did to her. I thought about all those times God tried to show me the truth and I just ignored it. It was God who kept me alive so that I could see the truth. He wasn't unfair, he only wanted love and loyalty. I had a choice to make. I could die…or I could choose to live. I fell to my

knees…

"Yes my son" Lucifer said "You have made the

right decision."

I fell to my knees, but to worship him. I

buried my face in the grass and began to say

the Lord's prayer…" OUR FATHER, WHICH

ART IN HEAVEN, HALLOWED BE THY

NAME, THY KINGOM COME…" lightning

began to strike, the storm was getting worse,

something was about to happen, I didn't

care…prepared for anything, I kept praying

"THY WILL BE DONE ON EARTH, AS IT IS

IN HEAVEN. GIVE US THIS DAY, OUR

DAILY BREAD…"

"DO YOU KNOW WHAT YOU ARE DOING!"

Lucifer yelled "YOU WILL REGRET THOSE

MEANINGLESS WORDS! HE WILL NOT

SAVE YOU!" The ground broke and a fire

arose and surrounded Lucifer. It enclosed

around him…I can still remember his screams,

I finished my prayer "AND FORGIVE OUR

DEBTS, AS WE FORGIVE OUR DEBTORS.

AND LEAD US NOT INTO TEMPTATION,

BUT DELIVER US FROM EVIL, FOR THINE IS

THE KINGDOM, AND POWER, AND

GLORY, FOREVER! AMEN"

The sky opened and I saw a bright light. At the same time Lucifer broke through the fire and charged towards me. Before he reached me, something snatched him back and shoved him under the ground along with the blazing fire that surrounded him. I looked up to the sky but it had already sealed. The rain had stopped and there was only silence…and then I heard a voice "I AM PLEASED MY SON; YOU ARE FORGIVEN…FOR ALL YOUR TRANSGRESSIONS…WELL DONE"

No one would believe me if I told them what happened that day, let alone what had happened the past year. I didn't know what was to come but my mind was clear. I stood

up, brushed myself off and started to walk

home. After a few steps I started feeling

drowsy again, I thought it might have just been

the after affects from the trans I was in but I fell

to the ground again…into another deep sleep.

CHAPTER 29

When I woke up, I wasn't in the middle of the football field anymore. I was sitting at my desk back at school. I was wearing a white tee shirt. Looking down I saw that my whole outfit was white. Ms. Kirkpatrick was in the front of the room teaching as if it were a normal day. Everyone was listening, taking notes and looking through their books. I looked to see who was sitting behind me and my heart dropped. It was Amy! She looked up at me and smiled before she went back to jotting her notes down.

I noticed Brad wasn't sitting next to her in his normal seat. Suddenly, a balled up piece of paper hit me in the back of the head. I looked towards the front of the class and saw Brad sitting a few rows in front of me. As big as a douche as he was, I was glad to see him. I quickly grabbed my cell phone from my back pack. I checked my notifications and couldn't believe what I saw! It was a text from Mark! It was a message reminding me that we were going to grab something to eat after school. The strangest thing was the date on my phone. Time had literally went back to the beginning of the school year! I opened my back pack expecting to see my Satanic Bible, it wasn't

there. Instead, it was the book that I should've

been reading the whole time...my Holy Bible.

The bell rang and everyone was

dismissed from class. As I was headed towards

my locker, I accidently bumped into someone.

I picked up the book that dropped from the

other person's hands. As I handed it back and

attempted to apologize I noticed it was the

strange girl with the nice glasses. She had on

the same white shirt and jeans as before. She

had a huge smile on her face "Hello Christian"

she said. There was a short pause "Aren't you

going to ask me if I wanted to knew the truth

or something?" I asked. She laughed "No" she gave me a hug and started to walk in the other direction "You already know the truth". No one seemed to notice her or acknowledge her as she walked away.

I walked the halls, still headed for my locker. I saw Amy and Brad talking to each other. Brad had on his varsity jacket and Amy was holding her books just like I remembered. I started grinning…I knew that it was the time where Amy and I were supposed to stare at each other. When here eyes locked in with mine my grin became a goofy smile. I was so excited that I forgot what was supposed to happen next. I suddenly remembered as my

head hit the lockers from Brad's sucker punch.

My eyes were closed but I wasn't unconscious.

I felt the same pain on the side of my face…just

as before. Everything was ok, until I felt a

breeze sweep through the hallways. I took a

deep breath, ready to stand up and face the

Devil again. I was helped up from behind, but

it was Amy. There were people still in the

halls, standing around looking at me. Security

took Brad away. Someone closed the door in

the hall that was letting the breeze come in.

"I'm sorry about that" Amy said as she

fixed my hair and adjusted my shirt. "He's

such a jerk, I'm Amy by the way". It was a little

strange listening to her introduce herself after

all we had been through. I thought about

telling her what happened, but what would've

been the point. Its not like she would have

believed me anyway. I just smiled and held out

my hand for her to shake "Christian" I said.

I walked away thinking about the past

year and my crazy obsession. I realized it had

cost me everything. It cost me my girlfriend,

the life of my best friend and even my

sanity...bit God allowed me to gain it all back.

For the first time, I felt complete. I was happy, I

had another shot at Amy...Mark was alive. I

even had the courage to make a few new friends. Finally, my life wasn't a mystery anymore. I knew who I was…I knew who my mother was and I knew she loved me very much. Most importantly, I finally knew who my father was…my real father.

TO BE CONTINUED...

ACKNOWLEGEMENTS

- JESUS CHRIST

- JOYCE GREEN

- WILLIE GREEN

- CHRISTOPHER HUDSON

- DILAN GREEN

- ROGER MORNEAU

- TIA POWE

- DANIEL RODGRIGEZ

- DR. E.D. HAYNES

- PASTOR JEROME HURST

ALSO AVAILABLE FROM DDA PUB.

CHOICE II – JAMES GREEN

JAMES VS DAREK – JAMES GREEN

JAMES VS DAREK 2- JAMES GREEN

JAMES VS DAREK 3 – JAMES GREEN

WHEN MY HEART SPEAKS MY PEN

LEAKS – CALINA BLACK

COMING SOON

SPARKLE – NONI BROOKS

www.ingramcontent.com/pod-product-compliance
Lightning Source LLC
Chambersburg PA
CBHW052038240626
47153CB00006B/2147